BLACK
FRIDAY

# BLACK FRIDAY

## TIM LaHaye
### and BOB DeMoss

W PUBLISHING GROUP™
www.wpublishinggroup.com

*A Division of Thomas Nelson, Inc.*
*www.ThomasNelson.com*

To Walt, Jane, Becky, Amy, and Ruth Turner
For twenty great years of friendship

He snatched the handset with his left hand. His right fore-finger, with the force of a woodpecker, drilled the keypad. He pressed the earpiece to the side of his head. Two hundred miles away, a phone in Maryland rang. The forefinger of his right hand thumped against the desktop with impatience as he waited.

A second ring.

His eyes burned a hole into the phone as if he could will the party on the other end to pick up.

The third ring produced an answering machine.

As he listened to the message, displeased by the failure to make direct contact, he blew a hard breath through clenched teeth. The tone sounded. He spoke two words.

"Call me."

He tossed the handset into the cradle with a snap. He checked his gold Rolex and frowned. As far as he was concerned, midnight always seemed to arrive too quickly. He ran impatient fingers over his receding hairline and through his white hair. There was so much to do and so little time left to do it. With a push, he backed his leather chair away from the desk and then swiveled to face a row of crystal bottles arranged on the credenza behind him.

As he reached for a glass with his right hand, he noticed the tremor was worse this evening. He stretched out both arms in front of him, keeping his palms down. He commanded his hands to be steady. A friend had suggested the maneuver as a way to maintain control. He thought the whole exercise was stupid but tried it anyway.

It didn't work.

"Figures," he said.

His lip curled into a snarl.

He stared at his shaking right hand, mad. Mad and afraid of the implication. The tremor had started as a mild twitch six months ago. Three months later, during surgery, his hand had slipped. He recovered quickly, although he couldn't be sure whether or not he had overcompensated. He was fairly confident nobody had noticed.

Not that it mattered. He was the boss.

He reached once again for a tumbler and then greedily strangled the neck of a bottle of bourbon. He poured it straight up. With a jerk, he tossed the drink against the back of his throat and, just as quickly, poured a second glass. Although the office was quiet now, the voices echoing inside his head refused to be silenced. He closed his bloodshot eyes and leaned his head against the back of his generously padded chair.

Just as his nerves began to settle, the phone rang.

He placed the tumbler on the desk, eyes still closed, and reached for the phone.

"Yes?"

"You called," the voice said. "What do you want from me?"

"I thought you were a professional. I pay you enough, don't I?"

The caller from Maryland didn't immediately respond. He cleared his throat. "A minor setback, that's all. We'll win on appeal."

"Just tell me this," he said, his eyes now wide open. "How could you let this happen?"

"It's complicated—"

"I pay you to keep . . . *things* . . . uncomplicated," he said, leaning forward. He placed his arms on the desk.

"Fine. I'll take care of it," the voice said. "Like I said, this is just a minor bump in the road. Nobody in Philly knows about this."

His forefinger resumed its rapid thump. "That's where you're wrong." He picked up a pink piece of paper from the corner of the desk and studied the name of the person handwritten in the upper left corner. His eyes narrowed. "Does the name Jodi Adams mean anything to you?"

The caller hesitated. "Can't say I've heard of her. A lawyer?"

"Worse. A reporter, of sorts."

"I see."

"Didn't I tell you secrecy is everything?" With a flick, the paper floated to the edge of his desk. "I want you to know I don't like what I'm hearing. Make my problems go away—or we're through working together. Have I been clear?"

Before the caller could respond, he hung up.

**S**tan's missing?" Jodi Adams sat on her bedroom floor in running shorts, her legs crossed Indian-style. The phone was sandwiched between her left ear and shoulder. She picked through the ends of her hair as she listened to the news. She fought the urge to overreact. "Like, what do you mean—*missing?*"

"It's really weird," Heather Barnes said. "All I know is his mom called me this morning freaking out all over the place. She wanted to know if I had heard from Stan. She said he hasn't come home in days." Heather paused. "Um, I called you earlier to see if maybe you'd heard from him, but your dad said you were out."

"Sorry. I was jogging." Jodi folded her hands in her lap. "And no, come to think of it, I haven't talked to Stan in a while. Guess I've been too busy at the newspaper. Did Stan's mom say how long he's been gone?"

"She thinks maybe since Saturday." Heather's voice began to shake. "It's so not like him, Jodi. You know that."

Jodi considered the options. It was the middle of July. Stan "da Man" Taylor, a classmate and star of the Fort Washington High School football team in Huntingdon Valley, Pennsylvania, didn't have practice until next week. And, as far as Jodi knew, Stan still hadn't pinned down a summer job—aside from cutting grass and odd projects for pocket change. Besides, neither option would explain his staying away from home for three or four days. Stan's mom was a single mother and worked long hours, which probably explained how his absence went unnoticed.

"Did they have an argument or something?" Jodi asked.

"Actually, no. Things have been pretty cool around his house now that he's been saved," Heather said. "The only thing I can figure is he got a call from Faith Morton last Friday—"

Jodi cut in. "How do you know that?"

"I called Stan on Friday afternoon. I wanted to see if he wanted to go with me to Ocean City for the day on Saturday," Heather said. "You know, get a jump-start on my tan. Maybe ride bikes up and down the boardwalk—stuff like that. That's the last we talked."

"I noticed you didn't invite me, Heather," Jodi said, pretending to be hurt. "I love the Jersey shore. Besides, if there's anybody who needs help with her tan, it's me."

They laughed. "No argument there," Heather said. "I just figured you'd have to work. Anyway, Stan turned me down."

"So, who's Faith?"

"Stan's ex-girlfriend," Heather said, her tone noticeably cooler. She cleared her throat. "One of the *many* girls he's left in his wake."

Jodi detected a hint of something more than sarcasm. Bitterness, maybe? "Okay, time out for a sec," Jodi said. "How are things between you two?"

Heather hesitated.

"That good, huh?" Jodi switched the phone to her other ear.

"I don't know, Jodi," Heather said. "I guess things just got a little too confusing for me after the prom fiasco. I mean, I'd like to think we can work stuff out, but—" Her voice drifted off.

Jodi figured her best friend must be more than heartbroken. She knew Heather really liked Stan's wild and crazy side. He was a fun guy. Cute, too. Not to mention he was probably the most popular guy at school.

For several months, Heather and Stan had been hanging out. They went to a rave party in downtown Philadelphia. A few weeks later, Stan made a last-minute invitation to Heather for the junior-senior prom, which turned into an almost deadly experience and led to Stan's decision to become a Christian.

Since then, Stan had tried to do the right thing as a new believer, at least that was Jodi's observation. He had been reading his Bible and asking great questions. As far as she could tell, there hadn't been any sign of a problem.

"Anyway," Heather said, interrupting Jodi's thoughts, "Faith broke up with Stan right before spring break, you know, before the houseboat trip with Mrs. Meyer."

At the mention of Rosie Meyer, Jodi's social studies teacher, a host of memories flooded her mind. The houseboat was one of those experiences in life she'd never forget. In her case, it bonded Jodi, Heather, Stan, and several other students together in a friendship that they probably would still share when their ten-year class reunion rolled around.

"Oh, you're right," Jodi said. "Stan was a mess after Faith cut things off. So . . . she called Stan, what, like last Friday? And now he's missing. You think there's a connection?"

"I guess. Yeah, maybe."

Jodi untied her sneakers. "Come on, Heather. It's not like they eloped or something, right?"

Heather remained quiet for a moment. "I'm trying to be serious here."

Jodi ran her fingers through her blonde hair. "Okay. So tell me, what exactly did Stan tell you last Friday?"

"Um, he said Faith was, like, in big-time trouble—with her dad, or at least that's the impression I got." Heather paused. "Oh, and he said she was pretty messed up—and that it was all his fault. He sounded kinda depressed, you know?"

"*What* was his fault?"

"He wouldn't say exactly."

"Do you think maybe she had an accident or something?" Jodi said.

"I don't know. Maybe. Maybe not. He didn't want to talk about it. And, like, when I pushed him, he just said he wasn't sure she'd make it."

Jodi pulled off her sneakers and kicked them under her bed. "Did you try calling Faith?"

"That's the weirdest part," Heather said. "I tried right before I called you, but her phone has been disconnected." Her voice dropped a notch. "I'm really worried."

Jodi stood up, stretched, and then said, "Listen, Heather, I'm sure Stan's fine. He's probably just confused right now. Maybe he went to his dad's—"

"No way. Stan hates him for running off with that bimbo."

"Right. Nix the dad option." Jodi started to pace holding the phone base in one hand, the handset cradled against her ear. "Anyway, Stan's a big boy. I wouldn't worry too much about him," Jodi said. She checked her watch. "Oh, yikes, I've got, like, fifteen minutes to jump in the shower and get to work."

"Hey, how's that going?"

"It's been a breeze," Jodi said, "considering they've given me a fluff piece to keep me busy when I'm not filing stuff. They say I'll have more assignments after the boss shows up. I think he's out of town schmoozing some heavy advertiser or something."

"Meet any hot guys yet?"

"Remind me to smack you," Jodi said with a laugh. "I didn't go there to check out the male species. I'm a *reporter.*" She enunciated the words with an air of feigned superiority.

"Yeah, and knowing you, you've already won a Pulitzer Prize."

"Hardly," Jodi said. "I'm a glorified intern at the *Montgomery Times* . . . who's going to be late."

She was about to say good-bye when Heather said, "Oh my gosh, Jodi. I completely forgot one more thing about Stan."

"What's that?"

"He sent me this freaky e-mail," Heather said. "Come to think of it, I got it last night—"

"See, I knew he was all right, wherever he is," Jodi said.

"I've got to call his mom and let her know. Anyway, it was real short," Heather said. "He goes, '*Please pray for me. I just can't get all the faces out of my head*'—or something close to that."

Jodi's forehead crumpled into a thick knot. She wondered if this was one of Stan's elaborate pranks. First he disappeared for several days. Now this. Jodi knew from firsthand experience that Stan was good at pulling off some pretty embarrassing stunts. But she quickly dismissed the idea, especially since there was something going on with Faith.

Heather cut in. "Do you think he's, like, still feeling guilty over the death of his little brother a few years ago?"

"Somehow I don't think that's it," Jodi said.

"Why not?"

"Call it a woman's intuition," Jodi said evenly. She caught a glimpse of the time on the clock radio as she spoke. "Listen, Heather, I've really gotta run. We'll talk tonight. Deal?"

"Deal."

After she hung up, a new thought about Stan's disappearance crossed Jodi's mind, but she needed to make a few calls from work to be sure.

Jodi blinked twice and then pounced on the brake pedal. Her tires screeched against the hot pavement. The car behind her swerved, offering both a blast of an angry horn and a hand gesture for emphasis. She felt her face flush and managed an embarrassed smile in return.

She didn't blame the guy for being ticked off. She had been lost in her thoughts about Stan's situation and almost missed the turn into the driveway of the *Montgomery Times*.

Jodi felt her pulse race to keep up with the sudden burst of adrenaline. The last thing she needed was another accident so soon after getting her Mazda 626 back from the repair shop a week ago. The little white car looked great considering what it had been through.

She'd had a crash while outrunning a couple of angry Russian mobsters a month earlier. The gash had run the length of the passenger side of the car, and her windshield had crumbled into a million pieces. Jodi's heart skipped a beat at the memory.

She pulled into the tree-lined employee parking lot situated several steps from the entrance. The building was a one-story, nondescript stucco structure built forty years earlier. At least that's the date she remembered seeing on the cornerstone. She turned off the engine and sat, hands gripping the steering wheel, long enough to control her breathing. She grabbed her purse, stepped out of the car, and then closed the door, still somewhat preoccupied by the near collision.

"Excuse me, miss."

Jodi spun around and faced a man who seemed to materialize

almost out of thin air. Her heart jumped at the sight of the unexpected visitor. *Now what?* she thought. She eyed him with distrust, not that she had any reason to be distrustful—at least not yet. It was the suddenness of his appearance near her car door that sparked her defensive posture.

She figured he was at least as old as her dad, maybe early sixties. His graying hair looked like a dirty mop. His beard, a scraggly bush of black and white hairs twisted together like a Brillo pad, was matted with saliva and food particles. His well-tanned face framed a set of eyes that seemed both intensely focused on her and distant at the same time.

But it was the suit that seemed most out of place. It appeared to have been tailored to fit the man, not just something he picked off the rack at Goodwill. The wrinkled fabric and the patchwork of tears and stains made the garment look older than it probably was—at least that was her guess.

She found her voice.

"Yes? Can I help you?"

He shuffled forward two steps, stopped, looked around, and then took two more steps. From this distance the smell of urine, mixed with a body odor strong enough to repel a skunk, assaulted her nose. Jodi clutched her purse to her side. She slipped her finger over the car's panic button on the key chain.

"Miss, I'm sorry to bother you," he said. His voice was deep and had an almost sad quality to it. "You work here, don't you."

"Um, I do, but I'm kinda new here," Jodi said, her discomfort growing by the second. She'd been coming to work just over a week and had never seen him before. She figured by now she would at least have seen him pushing a shopping cart filled with assorted treasures.

Come to think of it, she couldn't remember seeing a homeless person in all of Huntingdon Valley, probably because it was an upper-middle-class suburb bordering the northern edge of Philadelphia.

Of course, had she been standing in Philly, meeting a homeless man wouldn't have been a surprise. They were everywhere. Take your pick. But definitely not here. She pegged him as just another crazy man who grabbed at his crotch in public like some kind of rap star.

Jodi surveyed her surroundings to see if she could tell how he'd managed to get there. Did he drive? No. She was familiar with the six other cars in the parking lot. Bus? There was a bus stop two blocks away, she noted. Maybe. Didn't matter. She was due at her desk, and whatever this guy wanted, well, somehow she had to find a way to detach herself from the conversation.

Jodi figured she'd try making a big deal of looking at her watch. Maybe he'd get the hint. "Uh, look at the time. If you don't mind, I'm running kinda late. Maybe we could talk inside?"

He nodded at that. "Running kinda late," he said, repeating her words. "Late. Yes. We're all too late most of the time, aren't we? We don't want to be, but we are. Life is like that most of the time. We're too late."

Jodi looked around to see if anybody inside the glass front doors was aware of her situation. The receptionist desk, which faced the doorway, was unoccupied.

Not good. Marge was probably at lunch.

Then again, there were the security cameras around the building. Two were aimed at the parking lot. She wasn't sure if they worked, or, even if they did, she had no way of knowing if anybody was monitoring them.

*Calm down,* she told herself. *The guy's probably just a homeless man looking for a handout.* It *was* lunchtime.

"My name's Gus. Gus Anderson." He made no effort to shake her hand. His head just jerked from side to side, paused, then jerked back and forth again.

"Nice to meet you, Gus." Jodi bit her lip. "I'm Jodi. Listen, Gus, my boss is expecting me—"

"Expecting me," Gus said, his eyes suddenly as lifeless as a mannequin's. "One minute we're expecting, the next we're not. Expecting. Not expecting. Expecting is good. Do you believe that, missy?"

Jodi took a deep breath. "Is there something you wanted to tell me?"

He raised a hand to the side of his face and tugged at the ends of his beard. Several flakes of dried food floated downward as he played with the tufts of hair.

"Tell me . . . yes . . . tell . . . tell all . . ."

"I'm sorry, Gus, but I've got a job to do." Jodi offered a thin smile and then backed away several steps.

"Miss . . . ah . . . Jodi?"

She regretted mentioning her name. Jodi planted her feet so that she could, if necessary, make a run for the doors. "Yes?"

Gus reached into the folds of his shabby suit coat and produced a white, business-size envelope. He held the wrinkled item up to the sun as if looking to see if it contained money. A moment later, his hand outstretched, he offered it to Jodi. "Please. Take it. It's the truth. It's all in there." His voice was calm and surprisingly steady, with a hint of urgency.

Jodi hesitated. To get the envelope, she'd have to come within a few feet of the stranger. And why take it? What did this have to do with her? Couldn't he go bother someone else with his ramblings? Then again, it was the middle of the day. He looked harmless enough.

She took a tentative step toward Gus.

With some effort, she willed herself to lean forward, pluck it out of his hand, and then retreat to a safe distance. "Um, do you want me to, like, mail this for you?"

A look of bewilderment, like a dark cloud, drifted across his face. "I thought you said you work here?"

"I do."

He nodded and then scratched his head. "Why would I want to mail it? It's for the paper. Give it to the paper. Go on, Miss Jodi."

The envelope was sealed. She stole a look at the front of it and noticed the name of the newspaper was handwritten in block type across the middle. In the upper left corner, he had written, "Gus Anderson, MD." *Great, this nut case thinks he's a doctor,* Jodi thought.

"I'll be sure to give it to the right people," Jodi said. "Now, if you'll excuse me."

As she walked away, she could hear Gus repeating her words. "The right people," he said. "Yes, the right people. Not the wrong people. No. Don't give it to the wrong people. Too many people are the wrong people. Wrong people will keep things from the right people. Give it to the right people."

When Jodi reached the front doors, she looked over her shoulder toward the place where she'd just had the most unusual conversation of her life. Gus was gone. She began to think she'd imagined the whole thing, except the dirty white envelope in her hand was evidence to the contrary.

Once inside the pint-size lobby, the smell of newsprint replaced the smell of Gus. Jodi's eyes took a quick minute to adjust to the dim fluorescent lighting. She quickly stuffed the envelope into her purse, figuring she'd decide what to do with it later.

She walked through the maze of half-height, cloth-covered metal partitions to her cubical against the far rear wall. As she made her way through the room, something dawned on her that she hadn't noticed before. The walls had no pictures. There were no paintings.

No splashes of cheerful color.

No copies of award-winning back issues to motivate the employees. She saw nothing but the dull, tired-looking olive-gray paint everywhere she looked. The carpet wasn't much better. The thin, indoor-outdoor carpet was a drab medium brown, which, in an odd way, matched the yellowed ceiling tiles. Some were stained in places, marking former leaks in the roof.

Even the phones on the desks were ancient, probably replaced during medieval times, she thought. The one exception to the collection of dated equipment was the shiny new Power Mac with an oversize flat screen, situated on the desk of the designer.

Still, it was a thrill to be working for a newspaper. The people she had met so far had been welcoming, almost like a family. And Jodi especially loved the energy when the cubicles were buzzing with activity. With only two private offices, you could hear the conversations of a dozen people at any given time. The exception was lunch. During lunchtime, the activity dropped to a dull hum.

Jodi reached her desk, a small, metal thing with a well-worn Formica top. She tossed her purse and keys in the bottom drawer, flicked on the switch to the microfiche reader, an archaic, yet useful device that preserved back issues of the *Montgomery Times* newspaper. It sat on a stand to her left, which put her back to the room as she worked. She resumed her assignment.

"Let me guess, you're the star summer intern that I've been hearing so much about."

Jodi spun around on her swivel chair. Their eyes met.

"I'm Joey Stephano." He extended his hand across the cubical wall. "We're glad to have you on board."

"Jodi Adams," she said, taking his hand. She swallowed. She tried to remember what she had planned to say when they met but only managed to utter, "Hi, um, sir."

*Sir? Where did that come from?*

Joey Stephano's eyes were dark, yet bright. They sparkled against his olive skin. His black hair was trimmed short and combed to the side. His shirt collar, opened one button too many, revealed a thick gold chain around his neck. He wore khaki pants and a black belt. She couldn't see his shoes but figured they'd be loafers. He didn't fit the profile, at least not in her mind, of a newspaper editor—certainly not of the owner. He couldn't be more than forty.

Jodi remembered to breathe. "Pleased to meet you, too, Mr. Stephano."

"Mister, nothing. Call me Joey." He held her hand several moments longer than she had expected. "Let's take a walk. They've probably shown you the place, but with me you'll get the official tour." He smiled.

Jodi stood, hooked her hair over her right ear, and walked to his side.

"Have my people been taking good care of you, Jodi?" He put his hand lightly around the back of her arm and nudged her down the center aisle.

"They've been great, really, sir." She wanted to kick herself for saying "sir" again.

Joey stopped and then looked her in the eyes. "Let's get one thing straight."

She waited.

"When you say, 'sir,'" he said with that sparkle in his eyes, "I start looking for my dad in the room. It's Joey. We're one big family around here. Nobody has to kiss up to me—I have no patience for that kind of thing. Nobody needs an appointment to talk to me. Maybe that's how it's done at other newspapers, but not here. How's that sound?"

"Okay with me, um, Joey," she said, trying to conceal a nervous laugh.

He started to walk again. "Good. Now, as you might have guessed, I'm Italian. So, as a kid, I always thought I'd open a little hole-in-the-wall place, you know, with a name like 'Joey's Pizza.' Got a nice ring to it—am I right?"

She nodded, taken by his openness. Seemed like she was really part of the team, and it felt nice.

"Anyway, I ended up doing college—excuse me, I attended an institution of higher learning—got bit by the journalism bug, found I had a knack for words and telling stories. Got a job at the *Inquirer*." He stopped in his tracks and raised a hand as if to signal something of utmost importance was about to be revealed.

"That's my office," he said, now pointing toward the corner room. Glass panels rose from floor to ceiling. The outside walls had one window with a view of a pine tree. "It's nothing spectacular. Me? I prefer what's functional. I even had the door taken off—like I said, I have an open-door policy." He laughed at his own joke.

Jodi smiled in return.

"Basically, I arranged the building into two work areas," Joey said.

"Editorial and subscriptions, which is where you and I are, and, if you'll follow me . . . sales and advertising are on this side."

Like a duckling following her mother, Jodi followed Joey through a short, wide hall to the adjacent work area. Here, nine desks were arranged in three rows of three. Each identical. Each with a phone, a chair, and a Rolodex. Joey continued to talk as they toured the building.

"The big city paper wasn't for me. You're just a number." He stopped, leaned toward her, and said, "They don't encourage creativity. Forget about following your nose when you're hot on the trail of a breaking story." He tapped the side of his nose.

They walked slowly through the open room. "Anyway, ten years of that," Joey said, "and I'm looking for the door. Next thing I know, a buddy tells me this paper is going to file bankruptcy. It would be a genuine fire sale. I sold everything, scraped together the cash . . . and here we are," he said with a wave of his hand.

"How long ago did you buy it?"

Joey stopped by the doorway to the only other private office. "That would be, what, about eighteen months—am I right, Roxanne?"

Roxanne didn't look up from the piles of paper that buried every square inch of her desktop. Her fingers hovered above an adding machine. A cigarette hung from her mouth as a ring of smoke circled her head like a ring around Saturn. "Eighteen months, twelve days."

"Roxanne is our accountant. Oh, and Rox, this is Jodi Adams, our intern."

"We've met," Roxanne said, still without looking up.

"She's a sweetheart once you get to know her," Joey said to Jodi, placing a hand in the center of her back as he guided her down the hall. "Rox is a fixture around here. Got her when we bought the place. She knows everything about everything. But if she barks, it's probably because she ran out of smokes. She probably does three packs a day. It's a wonder she's still alive." He laughed.

"You mentioned the paper was close to bankruptcy," Jodi said. "How are things now?"

Joey eyed her with what Jodi thought was a mixture of surprise and appreciation at her interest. "Truth is, our subscriptions are up—I think we're at forty-five thousand weekday subs, with something like fifty-one thousand on the Sunday edition. Of course, the money isn't in the subscriptions."

"Really?"

"No. Little-known secret . . . advertising pays the bills," he said. "Classified ads, space ads, and something new for us. I recently began to test 'P.I.' ads," he said, leading her past the desks and into a smaller room.

"P. I.?"

"That's per inquiry. We can get into that later."

"Mr. Stephano—sorry, Joey? Can I ask another question?" she said.

"Yes, Jodi?"

"I was kinda wondering if the security cameras outside the building worked?"

His left eyebrow shot up. "Well, no. Not yet. Why? Somebody giving you trouble out there?"

"Just wondering," she said, taken by his surprise. "I happened to notice them when I came to work. It's no big deal, really."

"Actually, the previous owner installed them but never made the final connections," he said. "Which reminds me to get that done—"

Jodi was about to mention Gus when Marge the receptionist, a heavyset, fiftyish woman, waddled toward them, huffing as she moved. Her glasses rested on her heaving chest, suspended by a cord that traveled around her neck. Her hair was cut short and permed, but little loose strands floated carelessly in several directions as if pulled by an unseen source of static electricity.

"Joey," she said, not waiting to be recognized. "I got an urgent call for you on line two—from the bank." A second later, she noticed Jodi. "Oh, hey, Jodi. Sorry to interrupt you guys." Marge looked back at Joey. "So, what do you want me to tell him? You out of the office, or what?"

BLACK FRIDAY ✑ 15

Joey offered a broad, toothy grin. "Better take that. Tell Old Moneybags I'll be right with him."

Marge nodded, turned to the nearest desk, punched the blinking light on the six-line phone, and then conveyed the message.

"The joys of owning your own business," Joey said to Jodi with a sigh. He led her by the arm back through the room, pausing by his doorway. "Well, there you have it. Like I said, glad you're on the team. I've got another project for you to work on—we'll talk this afternoon. Me? Gotta keep the loan sharks at bay." With that, he ducked into his space.

Jodi retraced her steps back to her work station. She liked her boss. She liked his warm, down-to-earth manner. She liked the way he made her feel, too. She felt as if her being at the paper actually mattered. This job was turning out to be even better than she'd first expected.

As she sat down, something bothered her. It was something she meant to say or do. But what? Then it hit her.

The envelope.

She had forgotten to give Joey the envelope from Gus. At her desk, Gus's words echoed in her mind: "Wrong people will keep things from the right people."

What did he mean by that?

**S**tan Taylor walked in the front door of the Abington Memorial Hospital, an imposing brick structure that dominated several city blocks. It was the oldest and largest hospital in the area. Stan knew he had been born somewhere in this edifice a little more than seventeen years ago. This was the first time he'd been back.

He paused long enough to catch the reflection of his profile in the glass door. The image that stared back at him was a stranger. He thought he'd never looked so bad in his life. The stubble on his unshaven face was uneven and blotchy. His eyes were puffy, accented with enough red lines to give a bottle of Visine a real workout.

Stan stepped through the door and into an open but cramped lobby area with a brown tile floor.

"Can I help you?" a voice said.

Stan's gaze drifted to the nurse behind the reception desk. He looked at the palm of his hand where he had scribbled a room number. "Yeah, could you tell me how to get to room 513?"

"Certainly," she said. She pointed to her right. "Take those elevators to the fifth floor. When you exit, make a left and go through the first set of doors. The nurses' station can direct you from there."

"Okay, good," Stan said. "Um, thanks." He strode to the bank of three elevators, pushed the call button, and watched the numbers above the doors. The back of his neck throbbed, and he reached around to massage the dull pain. His body ached from sleeping in his car.

With a ping, the center doors opened. He took a step forward and then stopped. A woman in a wheelchair was wheeled out by a chatty nurse. The woman's arms embraced a newborn baby, wrapped in a pink receiving blanket, close to her chest. Stan couldn't take his eyes off the infant. Her little eyes were scrunched closed. She was so perfect and she looked so . . . helpless.

The doors began to close on the empty elevator. Stan jolted forward and stuck his right hand in the way, causing the doors to retract. He stepped in. He was surprised to find a fresh batch of tears welling up around the edges of his tired eyes. He didn't think it was possible for a human—for a guy, especially, to have so many tears.

He pushed the button for the fifth floor and then stood against the rear wall of the compartment. With a thump, his head fell back against the panel. He closed his eyes as the elevator, moving as slow as molasses on a cold day, pulled itself up the shaft. "I can't do this, God."

A heavy sigh escaped his chest. He hated the feeling of being so weak. He was, after all, Stan "da Man." His buddies on the football team would have a field day if they saw him behaving like this—crying at the sight of an infant. How ridiculous was that?

But he couldn't help it. He'd brought this on himself, and he knew it. There was no way to turn back the clock on what he had done. He wanted to pray, even tried to pray, but he wasn't sure if God would answer.

With his eyes still shut, the faces returned. This time they rotated in a circle, as if riding a merry-go-round. Although none of their eyes were open, the faces of the babies giggled and pointed at him as they paraded through his brain. One face in particular called out his name.

"Stop it, just stop it," he said.

"You okay, pal?"

The sound of the man's voice jarred Stan back to the interior of the elevator. With a blink, his eyes opened. He watched as a janitor, carrying a mop, pushed a metal bucket on wheels into the space. The strong smell of pine-scented Lysol assaulted his nose. Stan, so preoccupied with the faces, was unaware that the elevator had stopped.

"You don't look too good, man," the janitor said when Stan hadn't answered.

"I'm fine, really." Stan swiped the side of his hand against the edge of his left and then his right eye. "What floor is this?"

"Fourth." The janitor pushed the button for the sixth floor.

"I'm going to the fifth," Stan said as the doors closed. He folded his arms and then, hoping to avoid a conversation, decided to retie his Nikes. As Stan fiddled with the laces, the janitor whistled a tuneless melody. Neither spoke again.

With a scraping sound, the elevator heaved to a stop. The doors opened. Stan walked past the janitor, stepped into the hall, started to go to the right but remembered he was to turn left. He walked through the doors and spotted the nurses' station.

Stan placed his hands on the counter. He cleared his throat. "Excuse me, but which way is 513?"

"See that door behind you?"

Stan turned and nodded.

"Just go through there, follow the crossover to the next building; you'll see it halfway down on your right."

He thanked her, turned, and then made his way through the door. He still had no idea what he'd say once he got to room 513. Everything he thought of seemed so . . . so *lame*. He wished he could wake up and discover it was all just a bad dream. Fat chance.

This was no dream—it was a nightmare.

For the hundredth time since leaving the safety of his car, he considered running in the opposite direction. But coming today was the right thing to do; at least that much was clear. His sneakers squeaked as he walked along the freshly polished white tile floor.

He jammed his hands into his jean pockets as he ambled down the hallway . . . 508 . . . 509 . . . Each step seemed more difficult to take than the one before it.

About twenty feet ahead, a doctor wearing green scrubs consulted a clipboard. He looked up from his notes and spoke to a man whose back was to Stan. A moment later, the doctor put his hand on the man's slumped shoulder. With a pat, the doctor walked around him and then moved in Stan's direction.

Stan swallowed hard as the doctor breezed by. He managed a grunt to the doctor's "Hello." Stan took a deep breath and slowed his stride as he approached 513. Maybe it was the squeak of Stan's shoes. Whatever the reason, the man in the hallway turned around like a guard on duty. The instant he saw Stan's face, he crossed his arms and moved in front of the doorway. "I really don't think you'd be welcomed in there."

Stan froze in place. He recognized the man blocking the doorway, but the unfriendly tone was as frosty as it was unexpected. His icy stare shocked Stan, given what he knew about him. Stan regained his composure, extended his hand, and said, "Maybe there's been some mistake. I'm Stan Taylor—remember me? I came as soon as I could."

The man, stiff as a statue, didn't budge. He wore a powder blue shirt, sleeves rolled to the elbows, and cocoa brown pants. His tie was loosened at the neck. He stood as tall as Stan's 6'4" but was much thinner. A pair of reading glasses rested on the edge of his nose. He stared over the top of the glasses, his eyes narrowing.

"Of course I know who you are, young man. Frankly, I'd prefer to forget the fact that we ever met."

Stan's eyebrows shot up. "Um, what am I missing here, Pastor Morton? I came to see Faith."

Stan hadn't laid eyes on Faith for three months—not since their breakup just before spring break. Faith, in Stan's opinion, got her attractive looks from her mother, who had died while giving birth to Faith. He wasn't sure what she got from this man.

"Don't play dumb with me, Stan Taylor." Pastor Morton's face was as pale as skim milk. Two pockets of skin clumped beneath his bloodshot eyes, and his forehead was wrinkled into a maze of twisted flesh. His dark brown eyebrows, like two fuzzy caterpillars, hung low across his brow.

Pastor Morton braced his jaw. "You know perfectly well what's going on. This is all *your fault*. And you want to know something? I . . . I should sue you for this." His Adam's apple bobbed as he spoke.

Stan looked at the floor, unsure how to respond.

"If I were you, Stan," Pastor Morton said, "I'd turn around and march right out of here—and never come back. Am I clear?"

Stan's eyes rose and met his glare. He fought to keep his emotions under control. On one hand, he knew he *was* to blame. He'd never denied that fact. On the other hand, Pastor Morton was a *preacher*, right? Stan figured somehow that should have made a difference in his tone.

"In case you want to know," Stan said, his voice on the verge of cracking, "I . . . I'm sorry. I really . . . really am."

Pastor Morton said, "That's not good enough. Now, why don't you crawl back under whatever rock you crawled out from and leave us both alone."

Stan bristled. "Faith *asked* me to come. So, if you'll give me a chance, I'd like to see her—"

"Why?" Pastor Morton said, still peering over the edge of his glasses like an interrogator for the government. "What possible good would that do? You'll only upset her. She's lost a lot of blood and needs to rest."

Stan's chest heaved. He felt his face flush. This was already an impossible situation, and Pastor Morton, although justified in being angry, was only making matters worse. Maybe he should leave. What was the point of creating a scene? And yet Stan knew in his heart he just had to see Faith. Stan ran his fingers through his hair. "I thought I might, like, pray for her."

"You? Of all people," Pastor Morton said with a laugh. "Come on, Stan. Don't play games with—"

Stan cut him off. "You don't have to believe me, but I've made some changes—big-time changes. I really would like to pray for her."

Pastor Morton smirked, evidently unconvinced.

Stan took a step forward. "Now, with all due respect, you can either step aside—or, I . . . I can push my way past you. One way or another," Stan said, jabbing his right forefinger in the direction of her door, "I'm . . . I'm going in there to see your daughter."

For a long moment, neither man moved. They stood their ground like prizefighters sizing up an opponent. After what felt like an eternity, Pastor Morton took a step back.

"You've got five minutes."

Jodi tapped her knuckles three times lightly on the doorjamb. Joey turned around, phone glued to his ear. His smile broadened. He waved her in. "I'll be there," Joey said into the mouthpiece. "Six, Wednesday. Works for me. We'll talk." He hung up. "What's up, Jodi?"

She hooked her hair around her right ear. "You know how you asked me to research health code violations at area hospitals for that story Al's working on?"

"Sure thing," Joey said, sitting down in his black leather chair. He clasped his hands together behind his head as he leaned back. "By the look on your face, I'd say you ran into a problem—am I right?"

"Yes and no," she said. She handed him a report summarizing her findings. It filled less than a single page. He scanned the sheet. Jodi said, "After I showed this to Al, he said I should talk it over with you."

"This is it?" He laid the page down on the desk in front of him.

Jodi nodded. "Like you said, I made some calls, dug around for complaints from workers, even spoke to the guy in charge of enforcement over in Harrisburg. Seems the state is pretty on top of their regular inspections."

Joey picked up a pen and twirled it in his hand.

She said, "Plus, they make unannounced visits to the almost two hundred—plus hospitals in the state. Most of what they see are, like, minor violations. Can't say we've got much of an earth-shattering story here—"

"If this is all we have, I agree," Joey said.

"But I was thinking about another angle—like you said, 'Follow your nose.'" Jodi tapped her nose with a smile.

He laughed. "I'm impressed, Jodi. You're a quick study. What's this new idea?"

"Well . . ." She hesitated. "I thought we might expand the scope of the research to include health violations at women's centers." She bit her lip.

"You mean, what, like independent health clinics, walk-in centers?" Joey continued to twirl the pen between two fingers.

"Well, sure, and um, in particular, clinics where pregnancies are terminated," Jodi said.

Joey's pen stopped gyrating. "Okay, Jodi, have a seat." He pointed to a cloth-covered chair facing his desk. She stepped into the room, pushed the chair back several inches, and sat down. "Rule one," he said, holding up a finger. "No agenda pieces here. We're journalists, not activists."

"But, I wasn't—"

"Hold on," he said. "As journalists, we report the news; we don't manufacture the news. We don't let pet peeves drive our pages. End of story. Plus, I don't want to make the big mistake that other mid-size newspapers make all the time. You know what that is?"

Jodi shrugged.

"They go after sensational headlines on bogus stories to capture new readers." Joey leaned forward. "If we go down that road, we compromise our journalistic credibility. The next thing you know, we're a big joke. We'll start to look like the *National Enquirer*. End of story."

*Boy, he sure likes that phrase—"end of story,"* Jodi thought. Although she respected his opinion, she wanted to challenge his logic. Last semester during her junior year, Jodi was the state champ in debate and, at the moment, it was clear his logic wasn't holding up. Why would it be okay to do an investigative piece on hospitals but not women's clinics? She thought that seemed like a double standard and was about to say so.

Joey's face softened. "Don't get the wrong idea, Jody. I appreciate your creative thinking. And, if there were a credible story, I'd say, let's do it."

Jodi tilted her head. "Mr. Steph—, um, Joey?" she said, catching herself. "I honestly don't think this would be a . . . an agenda piece, or whatever. The reason I mentioned the clinic angle was because of some of the things I bumped into while doing my research."

"Go on." He started to play with the pen.

"Well, for starters," Jodi said, "I found that clinics where pregnancies are terminated are, like, rarely—if ever—inspected by the state. Maybe once a year, if that. Don't you think that lax inspections would invite abuses?"

Joey considered this.

"Another thing," she said. "I read that, for the most part, veterinary clinics are held to higher standards of sanitation than these women's clinics are—"

He shook his head side to side. "I find that very hard to believe, Jodi."

"Well, that's my whole point," she said. "Why don't we do a piece that, like, finds out the truth?" She folded her hands in her lap.

Joey put down the pen. "Let me ask you a personal question. What are your views on the unborn?"

Jodi didn't hesitate. "I happen to be pro-life—"

"Listen," Joey said, raising a hand to cut her off. "That's the position of the church where I sometimes go, too. But as a reporter, we can't allow our personal feelings to get in the way of our journalistic integrity."

"I—," Jodi said. "I'm fairly confident I can walk that line if you'd give me the chance."

"Really?" Joey said. "Give me an idea how you'd do that."

Jodi looked down at the stained carpet for a moment and then met his eyes. "If women are going to terminate a pregnancy, which, like I said, I happen to believe is a wrong moral choice, at the very least it seems they should receive adequate care."

He nodded. His fingers formed a steeple in front of him.

"So, just like we were doing with the hospital story," she said, "I'd want to find out whether or not these providers are, like, meeting minimum standards for safety and sanitation."

Joey was about to say something when his intercom buzzed. He picked up the phone, listened, and said, "I'll be right with him." He looked at Jodi. "Banker Bob's on the horn again. I'm telling you, the guy must be lonely—I just talked to him a few hours ago," he said with a laugh. "Sorry to cut this short. We'll talk later. If you'll excuse me."

She stood to leave.

"Just tell Al to table his story for now," Joey said. "Oh, I still say your clinic angle is out of the question. End of story. But don't let that get you down. I appreciate your spunk." He winked.

Spunk? Jodi knew she was being schmoozed and didn't like it. She thought she'd made some great points. She thought at the very least he'd be interested in what she had uncovered about the clinics. As she stood to leave, she heard Joey pick up the phone and say, "So, how's my favorite banker?"

She turned and then walked out of his office into a billowing cloud of smoke. Roxanne stood just outside the door, papers in hand. She placed a freshly lit cigarette between her lips and sucked deeply. Seconds passed before she blew a steady stream of smoke through her nose.

"Hey, Roxanne," Jodi said, fighting the urge to gag.

"Let me guess," she said with a nod toward Joey's office, "Gave you the first-timer's treatment."

Jodi tilted her head. "How's that?"

"Oh, Joey talks a good game—journalistic integrity and such," Roxanne said between puffs. "Probably told you, 'We're journalists, not activists'—and all that."

Jodi's eyes widened. "That's so weird; that's exactly what he said."

"I know, kid," Roxanne said, holding the cigarette in front of her lips. "He's given the same speech to each of the other interns. But there isn't such a thing as an unbiased reporter." She took another drag. "Take it from me, girl. I've been around this industry for thirty years. They don't exist."

While Jodi appreciated the encouragement, if that's what this was supposed to be, she was having a difficult time breathing.

"But he's right about one thing," Roxanne said.

"What's that?"

"The really good reporters do follow their nose," Roxanne said. Her voice dropped a notch. "And, honey, listen to me. If you think you've got a story, don't let anything stop you from tracking it down. Just stick to the facts."

Jodi nodded. "Thanks, I appreciate—"

"Hey, Rox," Joey said, calling from his desk. "You poisoning the mind of our intern? Where are those numbers I asked for?"

Roxanne offered a thin smile to Jodi. She puffed again and then walked into his office. "Got 'em right here."

ᔛ

Jodi sat at her desk and checked her watch. It was almost five o'clock and time to go home. She gathered her keys, cell phone, and purse from the bottom drawer of the desk. As she did so, she remembered the letter from Gus. She looked up and scanned the room. The full-timers were buzzing with activity, oblivious to her presence.

She pulled the envelope from her purse and held it for a long moment. Should she give it to Joey? Or maybe give it to Marge, since she handled the letters to the editor. Then again, maybe she should look at it first and then determine whether or not it was worth bringing to anybody's attention.

Jodi snatched up her letter opener, slit the envelope open, and withdrew two pages. Not sure what to expect, she was pleasantly surprised to see that Gus had legible handwriting. She placed the envelope on her desk and then began to read the letter. Within seconds, the room and the sounds around her seemed to disappear as she got lost in the narrative. These were not the words of a drunken homeless man. No way. If Gus had written this letter, he was a very smart man with an unbelievable story.

The more Jodi read, the faster her heart pounded. The pages almost felt hot to the touch. For a quick second, she lowered the letter to her lap just below the surface of her desk. She stole a look around the room before she continued reading.

Another three minutes and she was done.

Now what? She stared at the letter in her lap, too stunned by what she had read to move. Almost in answer to her question, Gus's words reverberated in the back of her mind. *Too many people are the wrong people. . . . Give this to the right people.*

"Hey, Jodi, what are you reading?"

With a jerk, Jodi's head snapped up. Joey, hands resting on the edge of her cubicle, peered into her eyes.

A silent gasp escaped her mouth.

Like the wings of a butterfly in flight, Jodi's eyelashes fluttered as she absorbed the sudden appearance of her boss at her desk. Her face felt hot. It wasn't that she knew she was guilty of doing something wrong. She fully intended to share the contents of Gus's letter with Joey. Just not yet. "Excuse me?"

A set of keys jangled in his hand. "I guess my star intern didn't hear me calling her name—"

"I . . . I—"

"Hey, no problem," Joey said, a broad smile framing his perfectly white teeth. "I called and said good-bye several times. When I couldn't get your attention, I had to find out what was so interesting. Call me curious." Another picture-perfect smile.

"Oh, right." Jodi placed both hands over the pages on her lap. "Um, sorry for not saying good night," she said with about as much conviction as a kid caught with a hand deep in the cookie jar.

Joey shifted his weight, keys jangling in hand, but didn't leave. He raised an eyebrow. "So, imagine this. I'm standing at the door calling your name. I got no response. Here were my choices as an old, hard-boiled investigative reporter." He held up a new finger as he ticked off the options. "A, she's ignoring me; B, she's in need of a hearing aid; or, C, she's engrossed in something really juicy."

Jodi laughed.

"Me?" Joey said, "I chose 'C' for juicy. So what gives? Give me the juice—unless, of course, it's personal. Then, by all means—"

"Oh no, nothing like that," she said, her hands still hovering above the letter like a mother hen protecting her young against a predator. "I was going to give this to you, um, later. After I had checked it out first, you know, seeing as how busy you are and all." She hoped she didn't sound as nervous as she felt.

He winked. "Never too busy for a juicy scoop."

Jodi knew she really didn't have a choice but to hand over the letter. She picked up the pages and, like a lawyer handing over incriminating evidence to the judge, she presented the missive to Joey.

Joey put his keys in his pocket, took the letter, and then started to read.

At first, she studied Joey's face, hoping to find a clue to what he might be thinking. As the seconds slipped into minutes, she began to see the weather-beaten face of Gus. His bristlelike beard. His discolored teeth. His mop head. His well-tanned, leathery face. And those peculiar eyes with that simultaneously focused, faraway gaze.

She blinked. Joey was asking her a question.

"Where did you get this?"

"When I came to work today," she said, feeling like a traitor, "a homeless-looking guy gave it to me in the parking lot." She wasn't about to repeat Gus's warning not to give it to the wrong people. She didn't know if Joey qualified as the wrong people—at least not yet.

"You got this from Gus?"

Her heart jumped. "Actually, yes. How did you know that?"

Joey smiled. "He signed the letter, remember?"

She felt like a kindergartner on the first day of school. "Right."

"Hey," he said, as if reading her mind, "for what it's worth, he's been coming around here with his little secret letters for several weeks. I'd call the cops and have the mental case hauled off, but I guess he's harmless. Come to think of it, he always manages to disappear before I can call."

Jodi's eyebrows crumpled. "So, you don't believe, like, anything he said in there?"

He shook his head. "Jodi, in this business we have an old expression:

Consider the source. Why? Your sources are everything. The better and the more credible your source, the better and more accurate your story will be."

"But—" Jodi fumbled for the right word. "But he seemed so . . . *sincere.*"

Joey folded the letter. "You know something? Charlie Brown is sincere—and he lost every baseball game he ever played. Jodi, you can be sincere *and* sincerely wrong, see?"

"Okay, so maybe that wasn't the best word," she said, flipping her hair over one shoulder. "How about something like *honest.*"

"What makes you say he's honest? You've never met him before."

"Well—maybe it was the way he, like, pleaded with me," she said.

He laughed and then waved the pages. "These are unfounded, wild assertions of fact. His accusations border on slander."

Jodi slumped against the back of her chair.

"Take my advice," he said. "Forget this nonsense. Forget Gus. Better yet, don't talk to him again. You'll only encourage him to hassle you with more of these . . . these groundless ramblings. Next thing, he'll say the president is an alien from Mars. End of story."

She folded her arms together. "What if I could somehow verify what he's saying? That would be a huge story, right?"

Joey tapped the letter against the top of the cubical wall. "Yes, it would be. Heck, it would be front page material, but, like I said, considering the source, there's no basis for it."

"So, why don't I just—"

He waved her off. "Look around. We're a small paper with limited resources. I don't have the luxury of sending you or anyone else on a wild-goose chase."

"I see," Jodi said, looking away.

His voice softened. "You want to know something? I like you. I think your honors course teacher was right when she recommended you for this position."

She looked up.

"Still, you're gonna have to trust me on this when I ask you to let it go." He checked his watch. "Gotta run. I'll see you tomorrow and give you a story you can really sink your teeth into. How's that sound?"

She forced a smile. "Great."

"That's what I like to see, a team player." He flashed a grin and then turned to leave, letter in hand. She watched as he stopped by his office and then headed for the parking lot. As best she could tell, it didn't look like he was still carrying the letter. *He must have left it in his office,* she thought. *Maybe he filed it—or tossed it in the trash.*

Jodi's heart sank. If only she had made a copy, maybe she could check things out on her own time. She felt certain Gus hadn't completely fabricated these things; there must be some kernel of truth to the letter. Then, like a thunderclap, a new idea bolted into her mind. What if she went to Joey's office and, assuming he left it where she could find it, got the pages, made a quick copy, and then put the letter back?

What would be the harm in that?

E xcuse me, Dr. Graham," Jenna said. Her voice filled the intercom.

Dr. Graham placed his glass of Scotch on the edge of his marble desk, a giant piece of two-inch-thick, highly polished tan-and-white stone imported from Italy. He checked his Rolex and then massaged his temples.

"Yes, what is it?" he said in the direction of the phone.

"You have a visitor."

Dr. Graham leaned forward to consult his leather-bound scheduler. He grunted as he scanned the appropriate page. "I'm not expecting anyone, am I?"

"No, sir, you're not," Jenna said. Her voice had an inviting air about it, at least in his mind.

"Good. Then let's keep it that way," he said, closing his day planner with a snap. "I'm in no mood for—"

"Pardon me, Dr. Graham," she said. "He claims to be an old friend."

It was the way she said, "Pardon me," that always got to him. She spoke the words in such a smooth, silky tone. Dr. Graham pictured her red lips mouthing the words. She wasn't a real looker, in his opinion. But there was a wholesome yet sexy quality about her that he found downright irresistible.

Jenna was twenty-six, single, and she worked long hours in his office—often ten to twelve hours a day. With a work schedule like that, he didn't think she'd have time for a love life. She'd been on his staff for

almost two years, and he couldn't remember her ever mentioning anything about a boyfriend.

He had planned to ask her to dinner several times but stopped
short, afraid she might turn him down. In an odd sort of way, he pre-
ferred to live with the fantasy of getting close to her rather than the
reality of being rejected by her. He knew enough about rejection. Just
ask ex-wife number one or ex-wife number two.

If only there were a safe way to break the ice. Come to think of it,
he could invite her to go sailing with friends. That would surely appear
harmless enough. Not a real date. But a good first step.

He was, after all, twice her age.

These things took time.

"Dr. Graham?" Jenna said. "Should I show him in?"

He blew a gust of wind through his teeth. He stared at the intercom and pictured her face. "What's his name?"

"Sir, he wouldn't tell me," she said. "He claims he's someone from
back home who wanted to surprise you."

Dr. Graham folded his arms. He slumped back in his chair and
focused on the ceiling fan as it whirled overhead. He wasn't big on surprises. In fact, he paid both his lawyer and his accountant handsomely
to avoid surprises. He ran a hand through his prematurely whitened
hair.

On the other hand, maybe he should just loosen up and see the
guy. That way he'd show Jenna he was . . . a flexible person—no, more
than that—he was *spontaneous*.

"Okay, Jenna," Dr. Graham said. "Show him in. But leave the door
open and buzz me in five minutes if he hasn't left by then."

"I understand, sir."

Dr. Graham stood and then walked to the window. When the
guest arrived, his back would be to the door—a power move. It was all
part of the intimidation game, and he was among the best. A quiet
moment passed before he heard the solid-oak, six-panel door open
behind him.

"Hello, Vic."

Dr. Graham, arms crossed, turned around and examined the man. A bushy eyebrow shot skyward. He brought a hand to his mouth as he cleared his throat. "I'm sorry, do we know each other?"

"Know?" he said. "It's not *who* we know, it's *what* we know. Knowledge is good—and dangerous. Am I right, Victor Graham?"

The visitor looked familiar, even sounded familiar, yet he was so badly in need of a shave, a shower, and a new set of clothes, Dr. Graham couldn't quite recall the face. He strode across the expansive office and was about to extend a hand when the distinct smell of urine and other assorted body odors smacked him in the face.

"I'm sorry," Dr. Graham said, stopping several feet short of the man. "It's been a long day, and I'm having difficulty placing your face."

"I'm sorry . . . you're sorry . . . yes, we're both sorry," the man said. "We seem to know a lot about sorrow. Maybe because we . . . we cause so much sorrow. Would you agree?"

Dr. Graham didn't say a word. For the first time during their brief encounter, he looked—actually looked—into the eyes of his guest. The seconds passed between them. Yes, he was pretty sure he knew this man. But if so, it was a different place, a different time.

Dr. Graham stiffened. "I'm afraid I don't have time for riddles, um . . . what did you say your name was?"

The visitor scratched at his beard. "I didn't say, Vic. You haven't forgotten your old . . . partner?"

Dr. Graham brought his hands together behind his back, primarily to control his urge to strangle Gus Anderson for coming here. It had been seven or eight years since he'd last seen Gus. His chest tightened over this unexpected development. The glass of Scotch on his desk beckoned.

Yes, that was exactly what he needed.

No, make that the whole bottle.

Gus had been his partner in Maryland; that was a fact he couldn't deny. Hell would have to freeze over before Dr. Graham would dare admit it. If he did, and if Gus made a scene by dredging up the past, then what? Surely a sane person wouldn't believe the claims from this homeless-looking bum, would they?

"Nice pad, Vic. You've done well," Gus said. His head jerked to the left, then the right, and back to the left. "I bet there's a boat . . . I bet there's a red Corvette somewhere with your name on it, too." The words were spoken without the cryptic cadence.

"I'm afraid there must be some mistake," Dr. Graham said. No way would he admit that, indeed, he had a boat, a very nice sixty-five-foot yacht, not to mention a brand-new Corvette—red. He glanced at the phone on his desk, wishing Jenna's soft, comforting voice would interrupt this painful encounter.

"Afraid, yes, afraid," Gus said, repeating the word with a solemn tone. His eyes seemed hollow, distant. "There's so much to *fear,* isn't there, Dr. Victor Graham?"

For a moment, Dr. Graham thought Gus might actually pull a gun. A crazy idea, sure. But not out of the question. In his business, that was a growing problem. Anything was possible with a person like Gus who was so unstable. Dr. Graham controlled his breathing and said, "Is there a reason for this visit?"

For a split second, a troubled look swept over Gus's face. And then, just as quickly, he morphed into a picture of confidence. He raised and pointed two fingers, dirt caked around the untrimmed nails, at Dr. Graham. "I know about Maryland. I know about Delaware," Gus said. He lowered his hand, turned to leave, and then stopped. He looked over his shoulder.

"And I know about Pennsylvania."

The two men locked eyes.

The silence between them crackled with electricity.

Gus spoke first. He spoke with a sudden burst of clarity, as if the clouds of insanity temporarily parted in his troubled mind. "So, Vic, who has the power now? I'd say your world is a house of cards. Care to fold your hand?"

The phone on Dr. Graham's desk purred. "Your appointment is here, Dr. Graham," Jenna said.

Gus smiled. "I'll show myself out, *partner.*" Gus took two steps and then added, "Like old times. No drink. No. You didn't even offer me a drink." That said, Gus disappeared out the door.

Dr. Graham raced to his desk, snatched his Scotch, tossed it back against his throat, and then wiped his lips with the side of his hand. He was pouring another glass when Jenna tapped on the door.

"Sir—"

"What took you so long?" Dr. Graham said, returning the bottle to the credenza. "I thought my instructions were for you to interrupt me in five minutes—not five hours." As he guzzled another glass, his right hand trembled, shaking as if stuck in a wind tunnel.

Jenna came to the side of his desk. "Pardon me, but that *was* five minutes, sir."

The way she said "pardon me" took the edge off his anger. Jenna didn't know about Gus, so how could he blame her? He felt the effects of the whiskey smoothing out his nervous system. He sat down, pulled his chair forward, and then rested his arms on the desk. "Do me a favor, Jenna," he said. "Don't let that man back in our building ever again."

"Certainly," she said. "I'll inform security, too. So, he wasn't an old friend after all?"

Dr. Graham forced a thin smile. "That quack? He's a confused man; that's all there is to it." He cracked his knuckles. "Now, about—"

Jenna stopped him. "Excuse me, sir."

"Yes?"

"Then I guess you won't care about this," she said. "Your visitor asked me to give it to you after he left."

She handed him a sealed white envelope. In the upper left-hand corner it read, "Gus Anderson, MD."

S tan stood at the foot of Faith's bed. As hospitals went, this was a decent-size, semiprivate room. The other bed was unoccupied. A heart monitor chirped softly on its stainless steel perch to her right. Her eyes had been closed when Stan stepped into the room and had remained shut since.

Stan swallowed hard. Her dad said she might be sleeping. Even so, she appeared as lifeless as a china doll. Her skin, drained of color, looked as washed-out as the bleached sheets tucked under her arms.

The dim, indirect lighting didn't help matters. Nor did the television. Although the sound was off, the TV screen, mounted above the foot of her bed, flickered constantly. It cast an eerie bluish light across her features, adding to her anemic appearance. Two IV drips, their thin tubes shuttling unknown liquid from the sacks of fluid to her left arm, were taped in place against her skin with white medical tape.

Every breath Stan took was laced with the distinct smell of hospital disinfectant. He felt weak in the knees. He hated this place.

Complicating his discomfort were the endless thoughts racing through his mind. He was having difficulty sorting them all out. The feelings. The emotions. The guilt.

The guilt was the big one.

He hated himself for what he had done.

True, he hadn't been a Christian at the time. He had given his life to Christ just three weeks ago. Still, three months ago he had robbed her of her virginity. The fact that it had been a mutual thing didn't matter. She, at least, had said she loved him; to Stan, her conquest was just another notch added to his belt.

The shame he felt, even now, caused him to want to run and hide. Just then, something Jodi had said came to mind: "You are a new man in Christ, Stan. When you got saved, God, like, threw your sins into the bottom of the sea."

And he *was* different. That's what prompted him to come and ask for forgiveness. A tear warmed his face. He walked to her side and gently placed his large hand around hers. Her skin felt cold, even ice-like.

His eyes drifted to the hospital-issued bracelet, a thin, plastic band around her wrist. He saw her name and tried to read the date of admittance but couldn't make out the upside down lettering. He gave her hand a soft squeeze.

Her eyelids opened half-mast. "Stan Taylor, what are you doing here?"

Stan's throat went dry. "Faith, I—"

Pulling her hand free from his touch, her eyes flared with an unexpected burst of energy. "I can't believe my dad actually let you in here."

"Faith, please, give me a chance. I have something I need to say." When Stan had told her dad in the hallway that Faith asked him to come, he'd stretched the truth. She had called—that much was true. But she had yelled and hung up before he could answer. He thought by coming he'd have a chance to set things right.

Faith rolled her head to one side, looking away.

"Um, look, I want to ask for your forgiveness, Faith." Stan put his hands in his pockets. "What I did was wrong—"

Tears trickled down Faith's cheeks. "I wish you'd just go away and let me sleep."

Stan looked down at his sneakers. He was a big guy, but he'd never felt so small. "I'm sorry you decided to get an—"

"Decided? Look at me, Stan Taylor."

Stan raised his head.

Her eyes, like an angry cat, glowed. "*You* broke up with *me*, remember?" she said. "What choice did I have? As I recall, you didn't want to have anything to do with me. Right?" She sat upright.

"Faith, I . . . I never knew you were pregnant."

She fell back against her pillow. "What difference would that have made?"

Stan shuffled his feet. "I . . . maybe if I knew, I might have stuck around—"

"Maybe—nice, Stan." She folded her arms. "You really have such a way with words."

Stan lowered his voice. "Well, for what it's worth, I can't stop seeing, like, the faces of babies floating through my head. And, every time I see a baby, I can't help the tears. I'm living with this, too, you know."

Faith bit her lip.

"Even when I sleep." Stan took a deep breath. He brought a hand to his chin. "The worst part is . . . I picture my baby crying for me to save him. But I don't. I just let him die . . ."

Faith searched his eyes. The beep of the heart monitor was the only sound in the room.

"And another thing, Faith," Stan said after a long moment. "Three weeks ago I decided to get right with God."

"You?"

"Weird, isn't it?" Stan said. A smile cracked his face for the first time in days. "A little late, um, as far as what happened between us. I'd like to think I would have, like, respected you more . . . if I'd known then what I know now."

Faith raked her hair.

He sniffled. "I'd like to think I'm on the right track. Got a long way to go . . ."

In what felt like half an eternity, Faith didn't say a word. She looked off into the distance, biting her bottom lip as if deep in thought. Stan started to shift in his seat, figuring her dad would burst into the room at any minute and order him out.

She reached out and took his hand.

He glanced over his shoulder at the door and then back to Faith. There were several things he just had to know. "Can I ask you a question?"

Faith nodded.

"Why are you still here?" Stan scratched the back of his head. "I mean, didn't you get this done, like, a week ago?"

She let go of his hand, then folded her fingers together. "The short version?"

"Sure."

"I didn't know what to do . . . or where to turn," she said. She pulled her dark, reddish-brown hair back behind her neck. "I didn't even know who to talk to about it. So I figured I'd just pay the money and be done with it."

Stan pulled a chair to the side of the bed and sat down. "So it wasn't done here?"

"No, I went to one of those women's clinics," Faith said. She looked down at her hands. "Anyway, they were in such a hurry. I was in and out so fast I hardly knew what was happening. Afterward, I was cramping really bad. I mean, my insides felt like they were tearing apart."

"Man, what happened?"

Faith pointed toward the box of Kleenex. Stan handed her one. She dabbed at the edges of her eyes. "I figured I'd take a warm bath, you know, to relax the muscles. That's where he found me."

Stan gave her a puzzled look. "Who found you?"

"My dad," she said. "He came home for a late lunch and I was passed out in the tub. I must have blanked out from the pain—"

"When?"

"A week ago, Friday morning," Faith said. "I was bleeding pretty badly, so, not knowing what was wrong, Dad rushed me here. Turns out that clinic totally messed things up. They almost killed me."

Stan felt his heart leap in his chest. "Faith, you don't have to—"

"Wait a sec; there's more," she said. "When I got here, the doctor had to do an emergency hysterectomy on me."

Stan's heart was in overdrive. "A what?"

"The doctor had to take out my uterus—" Her voice was shaking. She clutched the Kleenex.

"Meaning?"

Faith didn't answer.

"Please, Faith. I don't know about these things."

She spoke just above a whisper. "I'm eighteen . . . and I'll never be able to have children."

Stan felt as if he'd been socked in the eye. His face dropped into his hands. "Oh . . . my . . . gosh." He lifted his head, fighting back the tears. "All because I was—"

"Don't, Stan." Faith took his hand again. "You weren't the one who—" She cleared her throat. "Anyway," she said, "Dad says we're going to have to sell the house."

Stan grabbed another tissue and then handed it to her. "I don't understand," he said.

"Dad's just a preacher at a small country church," Faith said. "We don't have insurance for this—"

"I thought you said it was, like, the clinic's fault."

"It was," she said, scratching under her bracelet. "They're saying I was never a patient—which is a lie."

Stan felt the room start to spin around him. Why had God let something like this happen to her—to him, too? It seemed so unfair. He leaned forward and held her. His tears mixed with hers.

Faith whispered in his ear, "They claim they don't even have a record of me being there."

When Jodi answered the door, she recognized the white T-shirt and the faded blue jeans. But the guy holding the Papa John's pizza box hardly looked like the guy she knew. "Hey, Stan," she said, pretending not to notice the redness in his eyes. "Glad you're here."

"Thanks." He stepped through the front door of Jodi's parents' house.

"Gosh," Heather said, coming up behind Jodi. "You look like a train wreck, Stan."

"Good to see you, too, Heather." He gave her a side hug. "I haven't figured out how to put a shower in my car yet. Take me as I am, or I can go eat this thing by myself."

"Right this way," Jodi said, leading them through the hall toward the kitchen.

As they walked, Heather said, "I guess you know your mom is really worried—"

"I know," Stan said. "I just talked to her. We're cool now. Just had to be left alone for a while."

"Hey, let's eat out on the deck," Jodi said. She held the rear kitchen door open for Stan as he headed out to the picnic table. Her dad had mowed the yard the night before, and the smell of freshly cut grass lingered in the air. Jodi pointed to the counter and said, "Heather, can you get me some of those paper plates and some napkins, please?"

"Sure thing."

"Drinks?" Jodi said, heading for the refrigerator.

"Mountain Dew for me," Stan said, shouting from the deck. "Or anything nondiet—with bubbles."

"Ditto that," Heather said heading toward the door, plates and napkins in hand.

Jodi grabbed a bottle of water for herself and a two-liter of Coke for the others. She was glad Stan had called to suggest they get together. By the looks of it, he'd been through the wringer and needed a friend. *That makes two of us,* she thought. She was dying to tell them about Gus's letter—at the right time.

Stan called again. "Can we get started? I could eat the whole thing myself."

"Wait a sec, Stan," Jodi said. She snatched two paper cups, filled them with ice, and then, drinks tucked under her arm, made her way outside. As she sat at the picnic table, the wind chimes, a gift to her mom last Mother's Day, danced a whimsical tune in the gentle breeze.

Stan flipped open the box. "Hope you guys like double pepperoni and double cheese." He tossed a piece on a plate and then passed it to Heather.

"This is great," Heather said.

He handed Jodi a plate with a slice.

"Yeah, Stan. Thanks," Jodi said.

"And three for the dealer," Stan said, stacking his plate with several slices. A second later, he started to tackle his first piece.

Jodi reached out and held Stan's arm midair. "Like I always say, 'You pay—I pray.' Sound good?"

"Oh, right," Stan said, lowering the slice.

Jodi closed her eyes. "Thanks, Jesus, for my friends and for this food. Amen." She had barely finished praying when Stan was deep into the cheese.

"So, Jodi," he said, his mouth full. "Um, where are your folks?"

"Mom's at some women's group clipping photos for a family album, or something exciting like that—"

Stan's forehead wrinkled. "That's exciting?"

"It's a joke, Stan," Jodi said.

"Boy, you must be tired. Even I got that," Heather said, dabbing her slice with a napkin to suck up the extra grease.

Jodi said, "And, my dad's working late, since you asked."

Stan licked his fingers. "I never did thank your dad for being so cool about, you know, the big-time mess I got us into with the limo—"

Jodi cut him off. "Stan . . . duh! He knows it wasn't your fault we got, like, taken for a ride," she said, smiling. She could laugh about it now, but on the night of the prom several weeks back, the limo ride had turned into a life-and-death situation she'd never forget.

"Yeah, well, still," Stan said. "I wish I had a dad like yours."

Jodi picked the pepperoni off her pizza. "Did you ever think about praying for your dad? You know, to have a change of heart?"

"That jerk?" Stan reached for another slice. "Okay, so that 'wasn't very loving'—as you like to say, Jodi. But it's how I feel."

Heather said, "Maybe we should change the subject—"

"Or not," Jodi said, cutting her off. "I mean, he *is* your dad, jerk or not. Sorry . . . I don't mean to preach."

"You're cool, Jodi," Stan said. "It's just so hard to pray for the guy who left me and Mom for some . . . some loser *chick* he met on-line, you know?"

Jodi nodded as she took a drink of water. "It's weird," she said putting down the bottle. "I just had this conversation with Kat. Think about her folks. Her dad's in jail for selling kiddie porn. How whacked is that?"

"I know," Heather said. "That's really bad."

Jodi looked at Stan. "But God still wants us to, like, forgive those who wrong us."

The neighbor's miniature schnauzer, Violet, her ears straight up like some kind of bat dog, started to bark. Jodi, who had lived there most of her life, knew Violet was easily provoked by squirrels. Jodi had decided long ago that the squirrels enjoyed provoking the dog. "Violet, chill out. It's okay," Jodi said, calling over the fence that separated their backyards.

"Doesn't seem fair, does it, Stan?" Heather said, apparently sensing his resistance.

"Not in the least," he said.

"But that's what God's grace is all about," Jodi said. "Grace is . . . a gift. We don't deserve it, we can't earn it, and it's not for sale."

"Show-off," Heather said, poking Jodi's arm.

Jodi tossed her wadded-up napkin at her. "I only knew that because Pastor Paul preached on grace last week."

Stan wiped his hands on his pants. "Don't take this wrong, Jodi. I'd say it's easy for you to, like, say all of that because you live with a mom and dad who love you. I'd bet you never had an argument."

"Go ahead and say it," Jodi said with a smile. "You think we're, like, that *Leave It to Beaver* family on TV, right?"

"Maybe I do," Stan said, his chin out. He reached for his Coke.

"Well, you're way wrong, Stan Taylor." Jodi wasn't mad, just tired of the label. "Everyone has stuff they have to deal with—even me."

"Give me one example," he said.

Jodi thought a moment. "My mom, if you want to know, got an abortion shortly after they were married."

Heather touched Jodi's arm. "You never told me that."

"Yeah, well, the doctor told them the baby had a birth defect or something like that and they decided to—" Her voice caught.

Stan and Heather stopped eating.

With a tilt of her head, Jodi said, "I happened to be the replacement baby." She looked at Heather and then Stan.

Stan formed the letter *T* with his hands. "Time out. You're a what?"

Jodi pulled back her hair. "Mom says something like 40 percent of the girls who terminate are pregnant again within, like, six months."

Heather crossed her legs. "Oh, kind of, like, to replace the one they, um, lost?"

"That's me," Jodi said, folding her arms together. "So, I've had to deal with stuff, too. Like, I sometimes wonder if I am loved for who I am . . . or, am I loved for who I replaced?"

Nobody spoke for a long second. The chimes continued their soft, atonal song.

"How long have you known?" Heather said.

Jodi looked toward the house and pictured the conversation. "I found out a couple of years ago . . . when Mom and I had 'the Talk.'"

Stan and Heather appeared puzzled.

"You know," Jodi said. "'The Talk' about sex and stuff."

Stan laughed. "My old man just handed me a box of condoms and told me to 'play safe, son.'"

"I got a book," Heather said. "It was there on my bed when I came home from school one day. That's it. No discussion—not that I'd really want to talk about sex with *them.*"

"Yeah, well, my mom thought it would be best to be up-front with me," Jodi said. "That's probably why we're close . . . But wait a second. What's all this talk about me? I thought Stan called this meeting."

"Yeah," Heather said, turning to Stan. "What's been going on with you? We've all been, you know, concerned."

Jodi nodded. "And what's up with Faith these days?"

Stan, his plate empty, leaned back in his chair. He folded his fingers together across his abs. He coughed. "I guess, well . . . these last few days I've been dealing with what a big screwup I've been most of my life."

Jodi was stunned to hear Stan talk this way. After all, it didn't fit with what she knew of him. She had watched Stan strut like a peacock around campus their entire junior year. Everybody who was anybody wanted to be Stan's friend. His parties with the jocks after home football games were legendary. He drove a cool car and always had a girlfriend, usually a cheerleader, hanging on his arm. Even the upperclassmen wanted to hang out with him.

She had first met Stan on a personal level last semester during the houseboat experiment hosted by their honors social studies teacher, Rosie Meyer. She remembered how cocky and self-assured he'd been on that trip. Who could have blamed him? He had just been named Most Valuable Player of the school's football team, and then Penn State handed him a full scholarship upon graduation.

Ever since he gave his heart to God several weeks ago, Jodi had seen amazing changes in Stan. He was asking great questions and trying to read his Bible every day. He made an effort to ask for forgiveness from people he had hurt with his arrogant attitude, and he wasn't afraid to stand up to old friends who challenged his new faith.

"The deal is," he said, bringing his chair down and then resting his arms on his legs, "I went to see Faith. She's in the hospital."

Jodi stopped chewing. She swallowed. "I had no idea. What for? Is she okay?"

Stan nodded. "Basically, yes. See . . . gosh . . . I knew this was really gonna be hard for me."

Jodi thought she heard him sniffle. She looked at Heather, wondering if she had heard it, too.

Stan fiddled with his plate. "Turns out . . . I got her pregnant, like, when we were dating . . . and I never knew about it—the baby, that is."

Heather's eyes widened. "Really?"

"What a surprise, huh?" He ran his fingers through his hair. He took a deep breath. "She decided to . . . fix the problem—but didn't ask me about it," he said, looking at Jodi.

Jodi bit her bottom lip, too stunned to say anything.

Stan tossed the empty plate on the table and then leaned back. "The real kicker is the doctor at the clinic messed up—that's why she's in the hospital. The deal is, they don't have enough insurance to pay for a hystorec— . . . a hyster—"

"A hysterectomy?" Jodi said.

"Yeah, that's it." Stan's face looked pale. His heavily bloodshot eyes met hers.

Heather gasped. She covered her mouth with her hand. "Oh, Stan, I'm so sorry to hear that."

He took another deep breath. "Faith says the clinic denies every-thing, so her dad has to sell their house to cover the bills—something like $56,000."

Jodi shook her head in disbelief. "That is so wrong, Stan. Did she say which clinic?"

Stan rolled his eyes up for a second, as if searching his memory. "You know, she did. It was something like the Total Choice Medi-Center."

Jodi's heart almost stopped.

"I know the place," Heather said. "Isn't that over on Street Road? I think it's by that giant school bus parking lot."

Stan shrugged.

Heather nudged Jodi under the table with a foot. "You know the one I'm talking about, right?"

Jodi was too busy finding her next breath to answer. She was pretty sure Total Choice Medi-Center was the place Gus had described in his letter. She had to be sure, which meant she had to get to the office before the janitors tossed the trash.

Jodi stood up. "I'm sorry about this, but I've got something I've got to do. Um, you guys hang tight. I'll be back in thirty minutes, tops."

"In your dreams," Heather said, jumping to her feet. "Wherever you're going, I'm with you. What's so urgent?"

Jodi said, "I'll tell you on the way. I've just got to get to the news-paper before everyone's gone—"

"Got room for me?" Stan asked, standing.

"You guys are nuts." Jodi held the door open. Under her breath she said, "I hope we're in time."

Victor Graham sat at his desk, his door closed, the window blinds drawn. He stared at nothing in particular, caressing an empty shot glass with his left hand. In his estimation, the day had been a complete disaster.

First, there was the phone call from Maryland in which his lawyer had reported another legal setback. No, it was much more than a setback, and he knew it. He'd been blindsided by a bombshell. He replayed the conversation, still fresh in his mind, for the third time.

"Victor, the prosecutor has added additional charges—"

"Now what?"

"Criminal negligence and reckless endangerment."

He swore. "Based upon what?"

"New evidence—"

Dr. Graham swore again. "From where? Where are they getting this stuff? I thought we hid everything."

"We did. I personally shredded the files you instructed me to dispose of—unless . . . have you considered that there may be a leak in your office?"

"Not a chance," Dr. Graham had said.

"Victor, what about a plea-bargain agreement? I could—"

"Wait. Tell me first, what's the worst-case scenario if this goes to a full trial?"

"A hefty fine—maybe in the five figures, plus a probation period." His lawyer had spoken the words in a monotone, as if reporting the weather.

"What about jail?"

The only comfort Dr. Graham took from his morning conversation was to hear his lawyer say, "No jail time."

"Then, no deals," Dr. Graham had said.

"Even if the fine is substantial—"

"I won't negotiate with those thieves. *If* it comes down to it, I'll pay their lousy fine. But no deals."

Dr. Graham blinked and noticed he was choking the empty glass in his hand. He set it down on the desk before continuing to rehearse the events of the day.

As it turned out, his lawyer's bad news was just the appetizer. The dreadful appearance of Gus, who'd materialized in his office out of thin air like the ghost of Jacob Marley haunting old man Scrooge, really took the cake.

At first, he couldn't bring himself to open Gus's letter. The white, badly stained envelope had sat on his desk for the better part of twenty minutes. He had to fortify his nerves. With two additional glasses of Scotch whiskey down the hatch, he finally found the will to tear into the note.

By the time he had reached the end of the document, he was paralyzed with a fear he could almost taste. The last thing Dr. Graham needed was Gus rattling these chains from his past.

Not here. Not now.

To make matters worse, his right hand, plagued by that wretched muscular tremor, shook like a leaf in the wind most of the afternoon. Even Jenna had said it would do him some good to take the night off.

Maybe she was right. Perhaps a drive and some fresh air would clear out the cobwebs and, hopefully, chase away the ghosts. Dr. Graham checked the time. In thirty minutes he could be boatside. The thought appealed to him. He pressed a button for the intercom.

"Jenna?"

"Yes, Doctor?"

"I'm taking off now," Dr. Graham said. "Close the place up for me."

"Yes, sir. There's one more item."

Dr. Graham started to clear his desk. "What is it?"

"I need to remind you we're getting short-handed again. We lost several team members over the weekend."

He shook his head. He hated dealing with personnel hassles, especially hiring new people. The initial turnover rate was higher than the average in other professions. In his case, Dr. Graham knew a trainee had to make it through the first week of orientation. Most didn't. And some cried. He had zero patience for a new team member who got too emotional. What did they expect when they applied? This was a high-octane environment.

Deal with it.

The cool-headed ones, those in the freshman batch who made it through the first seven days, had five additional weeks of training. If they got that far, Dr. Graham knew the odds were in his favor they'd be on his team forever.

Like Jenna.

"Then just get them replaced."

"Sir, you usually—"

"Jenna," he said. He stopped to soften his delivery. "As of this minute, you handle it for me. I trust you."

"Thank you. Have a nice evening."

Dr. Graham lingered by the phone for a long second before leaving his desk. He took the back staircase down one flight of stairs and then stepped outside his office building, a modern two-story, brick-and-glass facility. He headed for his reserved parking space, his stride long and purposeful. Like everything he did, he moved at a frenzied pace, even now when he was supposed to be relaxing.

He prided himself on being a man with the energy of a tornado, always in a state of constant motion. When questioned by his employees about his unrelenting intensity, he loved to say, "Better to burn out than to rust out."

If he hadn't dropped his keys on the pavement as he raced to his car, he wouldn't have slowed enough to appreciate the colorful display overhead. The sun lay low in the evening sky, splashing bursts of yellow and burnt orange across the horizon.

He picked up his wad of keys and, with a beep, unlocked the car door. He slipped into the leather bucket seat behind the wheel of his red, Z-06 Corvette, put the top down, and then jammed the appropriate key into the ignition. Yes, fresh air and some distance from this place were what he needed.

Dr. Graham fired up the 405 V-8 high-performance engine. Like a juvenile in high school, he peeled out of the parking lot, hoping Jenna was watching. He could drive to Pete's Marina adjacent to Philadelphia's historic district in his sleep, and sometimes did.

He had picked this center-city marina because of its proximity to Society Hill, the bustle of South Street, and the prominence of Independence Hall. Not that he ever took the time to enjoy the shops, the galleries, the clubs, or the historical sites.

For him, it was a matter of image and status. His sixty-five-foot, state-of-the-art yacht, with "Total Choice" hand-painted across the bow, could be seen from both Penn's Landing and the Ben Franklin Bridge. The year-round access to the luxuries his boat afforded was an added bonus.

He stomped on the gas. The thirsty engine snarled as it shot the Vette, like an arrow, into the stream of traffic on Street Road. He found the night air against his skin invigorating. He breathed deeply.

Yes, Jenna was right.

This was the ticket. This, and an evening spent preparing the yacht for tomorrow's dinner.

One block before he hit the on-ramp for I-95 South, traffic stopped at a light. He reached down and tuned in his favorite radio station, a commercial-free satellite network playing nothing but the Beatles. The chorus from "Lucy in the Sky with Diamonds" filled the speakers.

When he looked up, a man pushing a shopping cart along the side of the road caught his attention. His heart flew into a rage.

*Gus?*

He squinted and then kicked himself for being so jumpy.

The light changed, and he tore down the road.

As he headed south, the city lights twinkled in the distance. The Beatles started to sing "All you need is love." He, in turn, started to replay the vision of Jenna's delight when he invited her to join him and several other guests on his boat Wednesday night. Her thick, red lips seemed to shimmer with desire as she said, "That would be nice."

He wondered what she would wear.

He certainly knew what he wanted her to wear.

He pictured her in a skimpy, low-cut gown with a long slit riding high up her leg. His daydream was cut short when his headlights cast a bluish-white beam on a homeless man slumped against the base of a bridge.

His thoughts returned to Gus.

Gus was a wild-card threat, of that he was certain. And while Gus might have appeared like an unstable homeless drifter, Dr. Graham knew Gus was probably still sharp as a tack under those layers of dust and scum. Left unchecked, Dr. Graham knew he could lose everything. His business, his home, his reputation, his dreams.

All because of Gus.

Why couldn't Gus mind his own business? Why did he insist on nosing around in matters that were no longer his concern? Sure, they had been partners. But that was a lifetime ago.

Why did Gus back him into a corner with that letter?

If the old fool insisted on his course of action, Dr. Graham knew he would be ruined. At least in the Philadelphia area.

Sure, he could always move out of state if things heated up. He had done it before. *Run, cut your losses, and live to fight another day,* he thought. But he enjoyed his new, custom-built home overlooking a golf course. His yacht. His slice of the good life.

And Jenna.

Although there wasn't anything romantic between them, at least not yet, the prospect of moving somewhere without her—all because of Gus—enraged him. What right did Gus have to jeopardize his relationship with Jenna?

Dr. Graham swore under his breath. He pounded the steering wheel at the thought. He refused to have everything taken away because a homeless man armed with a ten-year-old vendetta appeared in his backyard.

No. He wouldn't let that happen.

The simplest solution was to take Gus out of the game. Permanently. No ghostlike encore. No way back.

The more he thought about it, the more Dr. Graham knew he had no choice but to act, and soon. Who could blame him for defending himself against a crazy man? Gus had brought this on himself with that asinine letter. Period.

As he drove, the thought of eliminating Gus seemed almost . . . comforting.

Who would notice that there was one less vagrant?

After all, for Dr. Graham, killing was a way of life.

J odi handed the gas station attendant a five-dollar bill. She jumped back into her car, clicked on her seat belt and started the engine. "Sorry about the delay of game. I didn't realize I was, like, running on fumes." She flipped her hair over her shoulder.

"Hey, it's your crisis," Stan said with a laugh.

"Tell me about it," Jodi said. She pulled into traffic. In her rearview mirror, she noticed Heather gazing out the side window. "Whatcha thinking?"

"Me?" Heather said. "Oh, I'm still, like, shocked by all that stuff you said was in Gus's letter."

Jodi nodded. "I feel the same way. Now can you see that's why I . . . we've . . . got to get it?"

"How do we get in?" Stan said. "Want me to break a few windows?"

"As if," she said. "The janitors will let us in. I'm pretty sure they're there until 7:30-ish."

Heather leaned forward. "In that case, we'll be late."

Jodi, stepping on the gas, glanced at Heather in her mirror. "What makes you say that?" Jodi was a careful driver, but she could lean on the skinny pedal with the best of them if, say, angry Russian mobsters were on her tail, as had been the case a month ago.

"Your clock, right there," Heather said, pointing to the dash. "It says 7:28. We'll never make Easton Road in two minutes."

"Gosh, you scared me," Jodi said, her foot still heavy on the pedal. "That clock is fast by five or six minutes so I'm not late to stuff."

"You're kidding, right?" Stan said. "That would never work for me. I'd be like—"

"Hey, whenever you two are done blabbing . . . I just want to say I hope this Gus guy is wrong," Heather said.

"Really?" Jodi said. She slowed the car for a red light. "Why is that?"

"I don't know. Sometimes the truth is, like, too painful to face," Heather said. "I'd kinda rather believe a lie, or, actually, I'd, like, not want to know about something rather than know that stuff is really going on. Make sense?"

"You've lost me," Jodi said, looking back again. "What are you afraid of?"

"Look, if Gus is right, then something major ought to be done about it, see?" Heather said.

Stan turned halfway around in the front seat. "Right. It's like if I found out our football scores had been rigged all season. Who wants to think Coach Thomas was fixing our games because he's, like, part of some secret gambling racket."

"Exactly," Heather said, squeezing Stan's shoulders once.

"Wow, Heather, I'll give you a half-hour to stop that," Stan said with a smile. "Like I said, if that were true—about Coach Thomas— and I found out, I'd have to do something about it."

"Yeah, Jodi," Heather said. "'Ignorance is bliss.'"

"Okay. I guess that's where maybe I'm wired a little differently," Jodi said. She turned right onto Easton Road. "If this stuff were going on and I knew it, then I'm pretty sure God would want me to, like, expose it for what it is."

"Wait a minute," Stan said. "How do you know that?"

Jodi smiled. "I happen to have memorized the verse just lately. It's Ephesians 5:11—'Have nothing to do with the fruitless deeds of darkness, but rather expose them.'"

"Whoa—isn't that your building?" Heather asked.

Jodi hit the brakes. Her tires squealed in protest. She snapped on her turn signal to cross into the parking lot. "Arrg! I did the same thing this morning."

Easton Road, which ran north and south through the northeast suburbs of Philadelphia, was a stretch of four undersize lanes. Jodi had to cross two lanes of traffic. The oncoming traffic whizzed by inches from her door.

"Hey, we're in luck," Stan said. "Looks like the janitors are just leaving."

The traffic was heavy. With her left hand, Jodi shielded her eyes against the sun as she watched for a hole in the crowd of cars to make her turn. Her right hand squeezed the steering wheel as a knot of tension formed in her stomach. "Come on, people."

Stan pointed. "Um, Jodi, they've locked the door."

"I can't get across—" Jodi thought she had a break, started to make the turn, then jerked to a stop. "I hope you get a ticket, buster," she said to a hopped-up Jeep with oversize tires. As the Jeep passed by, the bass-heavy thump of rap music rattled their windows.

"Jodi!" Heather said.

"Well—the creep was speeding," Jodi said.

Stan leaned over for a better view. "I hate to say it, but now they're getting into their van."

Jodi's heart clapped away in her chest. She had to get there. She figured she'd be able to sweet-talk the janitors into opening the door for her. She'd only need a minute. The blinking of her turn indicator ticked away the seconds.

She heard Stan unlocking his door.

"Stan! Are you crazy?" Jodi said.

"Well, they're heading down the back alley," Stan said. "I'll run—"

"If I can't cross, you can't either . . . hold on!" Jodi said, getting the break she needed. "Finally." She peeled across the two lanes.

"You go, girl," Stan said.

The Mazda zipped into the parking lot. Seconds later, with the building to her right and a row of thick pine trees to her left, she had a clear view of the alley. Jodi stopped the car.

"I'm so sure . . . they're gone." Jodi's heart pounded.

Heather leaned forward. "Now what, Speed Racer?"

This time, Stan opened his door and stepped out. "Maybe there's an unlocked window or something. I'll check."

Jodi just shook her head. She knew even if Stan could find a way into the building, for them to go in would cross a line. They'd be breaking and entering. That wouldn't be cool. She could get fired, or worse, fined. She pushed the gearshift into park, lowered the windows, and shut off the engine.

"What gives?" Heather said, placing a hand on Jodi's shoulder.

Jodi unfastened her seat belt. "This isn't right. I can't just, like, waltz in there now. We're too late." *As Joey would say, "End of story,"* she thought.

Heather sat back. "Well, what if we were to check out the Dumpster—"

"We could try, but I can't say for sure that Joey threw away the letter," Jodi said. "Maybe he put it on his desk, or maybe he filed it in the nut-case file. We should just forget about it." Discouragement, like a thick fog, settled over her.

"There's Stan, jogging around the edge of the building," Heather said, pointing.

Jodi leaned an arm out her window. "Let's go, Stan."

Stan sprinted toward the driver's side of the car. He hunched down by Jodi's window. "Everything's locked. But—"

"Thanks for trying," Jodi said.

Heather gasped in the backseat.

"Try, try. All we can do is try."

Jodi spun to her right at the sound of a familiar voice. Gus stood just outside Heather's door, between the car and the grove of pine trees.

"Hey, Gus," Jodi said, now leaning across Stan's seat. "Guys, this is the man I was telling you about."

Gus turned as if to leave.

"No-no-no! Don't go," Jodi said.

Gus turned back around and then looked at Jodi, his eyes distant. "Are these . . . the wrong people?"

"Gus—believe me. They're as right as they come," Jodi said. "I told them about your letter."

His head twitched to the left, and then the right. He reached for his beard.

*Think quick*, Jodi thought. "Hey, maybe we could go talk somewhere . . . with you. How about we have coffee?"

"Go talk somewhere, with you," he repeated. "I could talk. To the right people, I could talk."

Stan walked around the front of the car and opened the passenger's side door. "Have the front seat, my man," Stan said.

The wrinkles at the edge of his eyes smoothed out as a smile found its way through the bushy beard. He shuffled toward the car.

"I know a really cool place, Gus," Jodi said. "Hop in."

**G**us, order whatever you'd like," Jodi said, placing her purse at her side on the red vinyl seat. "It's my treat."

Gus stared at her, his eyes distant as if he had heard a new word and was processing the meaning. "Treat. Yes, treats are good. Thank you, missy."

She had taken the quick trip three blocks up Easton Road to Friendly's, a favorite spot for ice cream floats and burger plates. She shared one side of the booth with Heather. Stan and Gus paired off on the other side, although Stan sat halfway out of the booth where the air wasn't as ripe.

A waitress appeared, stuffed the tip left by the previous customer into her chocolate-stained apron pocket, and then wiped down the cocoa-brown Formica tabletop with a rag that smelled like stale milk. She circulated menus and then produced an order tablet and pen.

Looking over the edge of her glasses, she eyeballed their faces, pausing at the sight of Gus. She put a hand on her left hip. "I'm not sure he'll be able to stay."

Jodi offered a wide smile. "Um, ma'am, we're, like, having a meeting. I'd really appreciate it if—"

"As long as we don't get no complaints, I guess it'd be okay," she said. "Drinks?"

"Strawberry shake for me," Heather said.

"Make it chocolate over here," Stan said.

"How about you, Gus?" Jodi said keeping herself from touching the damp tabletop.

Gus tilted his head and then flattened his hands, palms down, on the table. "Coffee. Black . . . Black is good."

Jodi offered him a smile. She turned to the waitress. "And I'll have a water with lemon, thanks."

The waitress scribbled a note. "How 'bout to eat?"

Jodi hooked her hair over her right ear. "What sounds good, Gus?"

He pointed to a picture in the center of the menu and then looked at Jodi.

"He'd like your Friendly's cheeseburger special," Jodi said. "The rest of us already had dinner, thanks anyway."

"Gotcha. Won't take but a minute." The waitress collected the menus and then headed for the kitchen.

Jodi folded her hands in her lap, unsure where to start. Heather crossed her legs, rocking a foot back and forth. Stan looked pale. Jodi knew he must have a lot on his mind, what with Faith lying in the hospital. However, at the moment, she figured Gus's odor was getting to him. For his part, Gus stared off into space as if none of them were present.

Several awkward moments passed. For the first time Jodi was beginning to think maybe this was a huge mistake. What if her instincts were wrong? What if Gus was nothing more than a delusional street bum? Her boss had told her to forget about Gus, and here she was having dinner with him.

Then again, if what Gus put in that letter could be confirmed, she'd have a front-page story.

Even Joey agreed on that point.

Three words popped into the forefront of her mind: *Consider the source.* Joey had warned her to find credible sources. Was Gus credible?

She looked across the table. Gus appeared to be in a world of his own. His head swung to the left, then to the right. His face was long and sad. It drooped like a saxophone. Finally, her first question appeared on the tip of her tongue. She hoped it didn't come off sounding rude.

"Okay, so, Gus," she said in her warmest tone, "I've got to put on my reporter hat here. My boss doesn't think you are a credible source. Why should I believe your story?"

Gus's eyes widened. He stole a look at Stan, then Heather before leaning halfway across the table. He stared at Jodi and then spoke just above a whisper. "These are the right people?"

She nodded. "Like I said, Gus, these are my friends."

"The right friends?" he said, still speaking in soft tones.

Jodi's face flushed. "Yes, Gus. The *right* friends. Now, if you could, like—"

Gus straightened up, his back pressed against the booth. His thick eyebrows narrowed as his pupils dilated. His sudden movements surprised her. "I know *things* . . . the things in my letter."

"How, Gus?" Heather said. "How do you know those things?"

He focused on Jodi. "There are eyes everywhere. My eyes. I saw these things. I *know* these things."

Stan cleared his throat. "So, what my man is saying is that he was an eyewitness—am I right?"

Gus rocked in place. "No. I was a partner. With him. My friend. The *wrong* friend. My partner."

Jodi couldn't believe what he had just said. He didn't mention a partnership in the letter. "Hold on a sec," she said. "Gus, you're telling me that you and Dr. Victor Graham were partners?"

He picked at the ends of his beard. "No and yes."

"I'm really confused here," Heather said.

"You aren't the only one," Stan said. "It's not a trick question, Gus. Is it no or yes?"

"Hold on, Stan." Jodi tried to sort out his meaning. She thought back to what she had read in his letter. What part of her question didn't Gus agree with? A new thought surfaced. If Victor Graham worked to terminate pregnancies, and Gus had been his partner, then Gus did, too. By the looks of him now, he must have walked away from his partner and a thriving practice in Maryland ten years ago. But why?

"Listen, you guys. I think Gus is saying two things. First, he's saying that Dr. Graham *wasn't* a doctor—or at least not a real one, right?" She looked at Gus for confirmation.

He looked off into the distance. "Not a real one. No."

"See," Jodi said. "But, he's also saying this guy was his partner, at that women's clinic in Maryland. That's how Gus knows all that stuff he put in the letter. He was there, get it?"

"Gosh," Stan said. "You think Gus was really—"

"Partner. Vic was my partner . . . in crime."

The server approached juggling an oversize brown tray. She balanced it on the edge of the table. "Here you go," she said, sliding the burger plate and then a coffee mug toward Gus.

"Strawberry for you." She dropped a shake in front of Heather.

"And chocolate for you, honey," she said to Stan with about as much affection as if he were sitting in a truck stop. She handed Jodi her water and the bill. "Holler if you need something."

"Good deal," Stan said, scooping out a spoonful of his extra-thick shake.

Like a vulture, Gus hunched over his meal. Jodi watched as he devoured his food. His lips smacked. His eyes buzzed with excitement. Several sesame seeds fell from the bun to his beard, joining the crumbs that had already been there since who knew when. She had so many questions.

"Gus, I'd like you to answer 'Yes' or 'No,' okay?" Jodi said. "Just to be clear, I need to hear this from you."

Gus nodded.

"Were you a licensed medical doctor?"

"Yes. Licensed. In Maryland. Yes."

"Did you perform abortions?"

He nodded. His face seemed to droop farther. "Yes. Pregnant, then not pregnant. Over and over."

"What about your partner? Did Victor Graham have a medical license?"

"No." Gus licked his fingers. "Not there, not here."

Jodi swallowed hard. She struggled to take her eyes off Gus's hands as he ate. She couldn't help but wonder, *How many unborn babies lost their chance at life because of those ten fingers?*

Jodi's chest tightened. She had never been so close to a . . . what? A mass murderer? Yes, in her view, that's what he was. Legalized or otherwise, life stopped at this man's doorstep for twenty years.

And she'd just bought him dinner. What was she doing?

*Be objective*, Joey had said. *How is that possible?* she wondered. Facts. Find the facts.

Stan cut in. "Wait. I've got a question. If he wasn't a doctor, what was—what *is* he?"

Gus stopped eating. He looked down. "Mortician. Vic was a mortician. Hired him . . . to help me . . . do the work."

Heather almost flew out of her seat. "You mean, you don't have to be a licensed doctor to, like, do an abortion? That's impossible."

Gus shook his head. "Happens . . . all the time. Then and now."

Stan's eyes glossed over. "No wonder Faith—"

Heather must have had the same idea as Jodi. They both reached across the table and squeezed his hand. "Stan, that's not your fault," Heather said.

"Not your fault," Gus said. "My fault. Yes, Vic is my fault." Gus started back into his fries.

A heavy silence settled between them. Stan pushed his shake away and stared at the floor. Jodi knew this was hard for Stan. And, while she wanted to get at the truth in the worst way, it was difficult for her, too.

For starters, she wanted to smack Gus for the pain he must have caused so many people. She wanted him to pay for what he had done. How many girls like Faith had suffered severe complications because people like Gus were too busy shuttling patients through their hallways?

A still, small voice echoed in the back of her head.

*Love your enemies.*

Jodi folded her arms. Love Gus? Love Victor Graham, a phony doctor who, as far as she knew, just about killed Faith? *I'm gonna need, like, some serious help with that one, Jesus,* she thought.

For Jodi, this wasn't about the pro-life versus pro-choice debate. She was pro-life, true, although she'd never carried a picket sign outside a women's clinic. She might wave to those on the sidewalks who did. But she could never bring herself to be actively involved.

Maybe it had something to do with her mother's own decision not to give birth to her first child. She didn't know for sure.

In any event, to Jodi, this situation wasn't about the legality or morality of ending life in the womb. No. It was about peeling back the shroud of deceit, exposing the greed, and revealing the incompetence of the people at the Total Choice Medi-Center that could cost women their lives.

At least according to Gus.

Jodi sipped at her water, studying Gus over the rim of the glass. She looked at a clock on the wall. "Listen, it's getting late. I really have just one more question. Gus, you said Victor Graham sometimes performs abortion procedures on women who aren't even pregnant. Can you prove it?"

Gus tugged at his left ear. "No."

Jodi's heart sank. No proof, no facts, no story. More like, "End of story."

"You can," Gus said, interrupting Jodi's thoughts. "You prove it."

"How's that?" Stan said, speaking without looking at Gus.

Gus, his plate now empty, leaned toward Jodi. He spoke in an even, low voice. "Listen, missy. Go ahead—suit yourself. Go to Vic's clinic. Tell them you could be pregnant."

Heather blew out a breath. "Right—"

"Let him talk," Jodi said, waving her off.

Gus ignored the interruption. "Take some of this fellow's pee in a cup," he said, pointing to Stan. "You'll see I'm right."

Jodi searched his eyes, trying to absorb his meaning. "Gosh, he's right," Jodi said. "When they ask for a urine sample, I, like, give them Stan's, um, *donation?*"

"This is so dumb. Why would you do that?" Stan asked.

"Because, Stan, you're a guy—guys can't get pregnant," Jodi said. "If they test it and say I'm eight weeks pregnant—"

"They'd be lying for sure," Heather said.

"Exactly." Jodi flipped her hair over her shoulder.

Stan leaned back. "Wow, Gus. That's intense."

Gus picked up his napkin and, with a blast of air like a small foghorn, blew his nose. He wadded it up and placed it in his tattered, grease-stained suit-coat pocket.

"At the same time, Gus," Jodi said, biting her bottom lip, "don't take this wrong, but, like, how do we know *you're* not the one who doesn't have the medical license? Maybe you're jealous of Dr. Graham. Maybe . . . well, you're trying to ruin his business. I've never heard of all this stuff—like, doing that procedure on people who aren't even pregnant. I mean, come on. That's nuts—"

Stan jumped in. "She's right. This is America. That would be totally illegal."

"Yeah," Heather said, not missing a beat. "How do we know you're not, like, crazy in the head—" She made a cuckoo sign with a finger by the side of her head.

"Heather! That is so not right," Jodi said. She jabbed Heather's side with an elbow.

"Well . . . he just sits there like this is, I don't know, like some kind of game, or whatever," Heather said. She crossed her arms. "Sorry. It's how I feel."

Gus placed the palms of his hands flat down on the tabletop. "How I feel," he said, imitating Heather. "We all feel. I feel, too, missy."

Heather shifted in the bench seat.

"I wander streets—yes, for years I wandered," Gus said. His face sagged like a basset hound's. "Still do. I keep trying to walk away . . . from what I did. From Vic, too." He tugged at his gray beard. "I don't have much time left. No. Not much time. . . . Time is not my friend. Vic knows too much."

Jodi felt her lungs constrict. "Gus, you gave Victor a letter?"

"Gave Vic a letter . . . today." Gus started to slide toward Stan. Stan moved out of his way, allowing Gus to stand up. His head twitched.

"Why?"

"Vic is my fault . . . all my fault," he said. "Thanks for dinner, Miss Jodi. At least the right people know. Good-bye."

The black Ford Taurus was parked, windows up, engine running, across the street from Friendly's. Two men sat low in the front seat, their visors pulled down. The air conditioning pumped a smooth blast of cold air into the compartment. Although the sun had all but disappeared, the outside temperature hovered in the mid-seventies, and neither man cared for the humidity.

The driver, his seat in a semi-reclined position, maintained a clear view of the restaurant's exit. He wore an inexpensive, charcoal gray suit. His white shirt was unbuttoned at the top, tie loosened around his neck.

His partner, dressed in similar fashion, studied the screen of a Web-linked Palm Pilot. A small red dot flashed in place on a street map coinciding with their present position. He noticed the time.

"Say, he's been in there quite awhile."

The driver stretched his arms over the steering wheel. "You can say that again."

"Maybe too long?"

"Nah," the driver said, suppressing a yawn. "He's probably packing down some serious chow."

"I don't know. Maybe I should take a look."

"Suit yourself." The driver glanced over at his partner's handheld device. He reached across the car and pointed to the red blip generated by the Global Positioning System. "Isn't that his marker on your GPS thingy?"

"It is . . ."

"Then I'd say don't sweat it." Several seconds later, the driver's cell phone vibrated in his pocket. He fished it out and then flipped it open. "Yes?"

He listened.

"No, not yet. We should be grabbing him any minute."

As he listened again, his eyes drifted over the end of the car's hood to the exit door.

"Yeah, he's still wearing the transmitter. We tracked him to an ice-cream joint off Easton Road."

He watched a customer shuffle out of the building.

"Gotta run—I'll call you back. Our man's on the move. We'll talk when I have something." He snapped the phone shut, readjusted his seat to a driving position, and then engaged the transmission. "It's showtime."

His partner placed the GPS locator in the glove compartment and raised his seat. "You think he'll cooperate?"

The driver snickered. "What choice does he have?"

"Kinda makes me sorry for the old man," the passenger said. "How about I do the talkin' this time? You come down a little too hard on him . . . at least that's my view."

"How about you stick a sock in it," the driver said, maneuvering the Ford across Easton Road and then into the parking lot. He idled near the left corner of the building.

Gus wandered toward the car and tried to peer through the tinted glass.

The driver cracked his window. "Did you miss us, Gus? Let's go for a ride. And make it quick."

Gus looked to the left, then the right, and then froze.

"Listen, Gus," the driver said. "We've got just a few questions, and we can do this the easy way or the hard way. It's your choice. What'll it be today?"

Gus pulled at the ends of his beard, his mop of hair matted against his forehead. His skin was moist from the humidity. An overhead flickering sodium-vapor lamp made him look like an extra in a classic monster flick. A long second passed.

"Come on, Gus; have a seat in back."

Gus shuffled to the rear door, opened it, and sat down.

The driver pulled out the back of the lot and then down an alley to a side street, talking as he drove. "So, Gus, what do you have for us? It's been, what, a week since our last chat?"

Gus stared into the night, his eyes as dark and empty as the evening sky. "One week."

"How about you tell me something I don't know, Gus," the driver said, now heading east on Easton Road.

No answer.

"Say, Gus, I think you're stalling. What do you have to say about that?" The driver looked over at his partner, who stared straight ahead, refusing to encourage a verbal clash with Gus. "You've had plenty of time to dig up something—or have you forgotten our little arrangement?"

Gus blew his nose. "Now . . . the right people know . . . at the paper. . . . The wrong people know, too."

The driver checked his mirror, slowed, and pulled to a stop on the shoulder of the road. He adjusted the mirror. "Gus, what are you saying? Try plain English tonight."

"Plain English," Gus said.

"Right, that's what I need from you, Gus."

"Vic knows. I saw Vic."

This time the partners exchanged a look. The driver spoke. "Gus, I'm not so sure that was a good idea. You should have at least talked to us first. What did he say?"

Gus scratched the side of his neck. "Nothing."

"Yeah, and I'm Santa Claus," the driver said, and then pointed to his partner. "This here is Mrs. Claus. Get real, Gus. You show up after all these years and you expect me to believe he had no reaction?"

Even in the air-conditioned car, Gus's forehead was dripping with sweat. "Only fear. I saw fear . . . in his eyes. And rage. Vic is mad enough . . . to kill me."

Jodi made the turn into her neighborhood. "Heather, so why are you so skeptical?"

Heather, riding in back, crossed her arms. "I never actually said that I *don't* believe him . . . All I said is I don't *want* to believe him."

"Fair enough," Jodi said. "And, Stan, it seems you're not sure what to think, right?"

"All I know is, after you said what's in that letter, I'm mad enough right now to do something stupid—"

"Like what?"

"For starters, I'd put Dr. Graham in an old-fashioned headlock and let him taste the ground for a while," Stan said.

"Based on what?" Jodi surprised herself with the question. She was starting to sound like Joey.

"Well, on the things Gus said. I'm starting to think that's enough for me," Stan said, scratching his chin.

"What if he's wrong?" Jodi said. "I'm not saying he is. But listen, I've got a better idea than just bashing Dr. Graham's face in the dirt. If you *really* want to help Faith—"

"I do, in a big way."

"And if you, Heather, want to find out the truth as much as I do," Jodi said with a glance over her shoulder.

"Sure, maybe—"

"Then here's my idea." Jodi pulled the car into her driveway and shut off the engine. "First thing tomorrow, Stan, go get a job at that Total Choice place—"

"Now who's crazy?" Stan said.

"For real; I'm serious. You don't have a summer job yet, so why not?"

"Doing what?"

"Beats me," Jodi said with a shrug. "Maybe taking out the trash—I dunno . . . or be a janitor. I'm sure if a buff dude like you applied, they'd find something."

Stan laughed. "So, say I did, how does that help Faith?"

"You'd be on the inside," Jodi said. "You can maybe see things for yourself that back up what Gus wrote in the letter. Plus, that way I'll have another credible source for a story that could expose all the secret stuff going on behind the scenes."

Stan considered this.

Heather said, "What would I do? That is, *if* I agreed to help with your little plan."

"I'll tell you, but don't go jumping down my throat," Jodi said, turning around in her seat. "Okay?"

"I'm all ears," Heather said with a smirk.

Jodi smirked right back. "I want you to set up an appointment to terminate a pregnancy."

"Whose?"

"Yours."

Heather raked her hair. "Now I *know* you're seriously whacked in the head."

"Hear me out; I'm dead serious—"

"Me? Pretend I'm pregnant? Get real. No way, Jodi Adams." Heather brought her purse to her lap. She opened her door and started to step out. "I can't believe we're having this conversation."

"Fine. I'll do it myself," Jodi said. She got out and, with a *thwack,* closed her door. The motion-sensing light mounted by the garage door clicked on, tossing its yellowish beam in her direction.

"Wait a minute—," Heather said. She walked around the rear of the car to Jodi's side. She softened a notch. "I'm not saying I don't want to help you. Just not that part. Besides, I'm a lousy actor."

Stan, getting out on his side of the car, said, "Well, then why don't you go with me and we'll get a job together." He walked around the front bumper to join the others. "You know, maybe you could work the front desk or answer phones—stuff like that."

Heather looked up at the moon. "You guys make it sound like we're going to get a job at McDonald's or something. What makes you think they're even hiring?"

"I don't. But I say it's worth a try." Jodi winked at Stan. "This isn't forever, Heather. You can always quit after the first day if you want."

"That's if I don't blow my cover first." She reached in her purse for a piece of gum and tossed it in her mouth.

"You'll be cool," Stan said. "So, Jodi. Let's say we get in. What's the goal?"

Jodi thought a moment. Gus had said so many things in his letter. There would be no way they could prove everything. She'd have to narrow down the list. "Okay, let's start with the things you probably can't prove, like, that Dr. Graham isn't a licensed medical doctor."

Heather blew and popped a bubble. "I'm sure your buddy Gus has to be wrong about that detail. I mean, how in the world could Dr. Graham's clinic be allowed to stay open even one day if he's back there working on people without a license?"

"Heather, chill," Jodi said. "I didn't say I agreed with Gus. I have no idea if Dr. Graham's legit or not."

"Wait a sec," Stan said. "Is there a way to check stuff like that online? You know, maybe there's some medical board—"

"Good idea. I'll look into that at work," Jodi said. "My point is, you won't find out if he is or isn't a certified doctor by just walking around the clinic . . . unless you ask a whole bunch of seriously uncool questions."

"Hey, you know what?" Stan said. "My sports doc has his license posted on the wall. I've seen it. I could look for something like that."

"Yeah," Jodi said, "but I doubt you'll find one. And another thing, Gus said none of Dr. Graham's 'medical assistants' are actually licensed nurses."

Heather grabbed Jodi's arm. "You didn't tell us that before."

Jodi smiled. "I just remembered that part."

"Gosh . . ." Heather shook her head. "That's nuts," she said, chewing her gum.

Stan said, "Are you sure? If they're not real nurses, what are they?"

"Well, according to Gus," Jodi said, looking at Stan and then Heather, "Dr. Graham likes to hire, um, . . . women from, quote, 'the lower socioeconomic class' who, for whatever reason, couldn't make it as a nurse. In some cases, they just worked in a doctor's office somewhere."

Heather leaned against the car. "Why not hire the real thing? Is he trying to save money?"

"Nope. It's one word," Jodi said. "Accountability."

Heather shook her head as if Jodi were talking about the quantum theory of physics.

"Look at it this way," Jodi said. "If a new assistant doesn't have a medical background and Dr. Graham gets to train them, he's the expert in their eyes, see?"

"Not really," Heather said, raising an eyebrow.

"In other words, what he says, goes," Jodi said, hooking her hair over one ear. "And these assistants wouldn't know any different."

"Makes sense," Stan said. "There wouldn't be anyone to, like, challenge the doc if he wasn't doing something by the book when he's doing a procedure."

"Exactly," Jodi said. "Plus, he pays them top dollar—as if they were nurses—so they have no reason to leave."

Stan whistled. "Makes me wonder how many other clinics are like that, you know?"

"Uh-huh. That's why this could be such a big story," Jodi said, smacking a gnat against her arm. "And, remember, Gus did the same thing in Maryland when he and Dr. Graham were partners, or so he says."

"Well, if those are the things we can't check out," Heather said, "what would we look for—again, *if* I were convinced to help out?"

"I'd say there are two main things," Jodi said. "First, we've got to see if, like Gus said, they're giving out those low-dose birth-control pills."

"I find that so hard to believe," Heather said.

"Hey, I'm male," Stan said. "What's that got to do with anything?"

"Stan, you're a brain-dead male," Jodi said, punching him lightly in the arm. "How many teens do you know who do, like, the same thing exactly the same way at the same time every day?"

Stan rubbed his arm. "I'd say not many."

"Right. And, because the pills they supposedly give out are of such a low dosage," Jodi said, "they've got to be taken exactly the same way and the same time every day or they won't offer any real protection against a future pregnancy."

"Says who?" Heather said, popping her gum.

"Gus."

Stan whistled. "Wow. So a kid goes in, gets the free pills—"

"Low-dose pills," Jodi said. "Unlike the normal prescription kind."

"Right," Stan said, "then they do the wild thing thinking they're not gonna get prego. But—bam—the next thing they know, they're headed back to the clinic—"

"All because they messed up their schedule," Jodi said.

"That means big-time repeat business for the doc," Stan said, ramming a fist into the palm of his other hand. "Now I really want to tackle that scumbag."

Heather folded her arms. "Seems far-fetched."

"Maybe. We'll try to find out for sure. Anyway," Jodi said, "the second thing you'd need to do is kinda hard to even talk about. We, um, need to find out what happens to the babies' remains."

"This is so gross," Heather said, holding herself as if chilled.

"I know." Jodi swallowed hard, then stole a look at Stan. Up until now, Stan seemed engaged, even energized by the prospect of doing a little undercover work. At the same time, she knew this wouldn't be easy for Stan to hear, especially since Faith had just undergone the procedure and he was still obviously shaken up about it.

Stan interrupted her thoughts. He had a faraway look in his eyes. "Don't most clinics just toss them down the garbage disposal?"

"Yes," she said, surprised by his observation. She wondered how he knew that but wasn't about to ask. "Um, what we need to find out is if some of . . . of the bodies are packaged and shipped out to labs for—" Jodi stopped. She took a deep breath. "I'm sorry, Stan, maybe this isn't such a good idea to—"

"Jodi . . . " He gave her an extended side hug. His bloodshot eyes shimmered with a fresh wetness. He sniffled. "I'm okay. Go on . . ."

"Are you sure?" She searched his eyes.

"Yeah. I mean, if anything," Stan said, clearing his throat, "what I can't handle is the thought that I might, like, meet that lady with the list. I swear, I'll lose it."

On the way to the newspaper earlier that evening, Jodi told them about the List Lady. In his letter, Gus described a woman who operated as a middleman. She arrived at the clinic once a week with a list of baby parts from fetuses eighteen to twenty-four weeks old, as if she were going to the meat department looking for specific cuts of beef.

Gus claimed she represented various research labs, fetal tissue banks, and "technology-driven, specialty cosmetic companies." Ever since she'd read that in Gus's letter, Jodi had struggled with a heavy sadness. She couldn't imagine anything so horrible.

Jodi wiped the edges of her eyes. "Look, if she exists—and I pray she doesn't—you'd be verifying something extremely important from Gus's letter."

"I don't know, guys," Heather said, shaking her head. "This is all so unreal. I mean, I read a Robin Cook novel once. He does those medical thrillers. Anyway, this sounds like something he'd dream up."

"Suppose for a second you're right," Jodi said, pulling her hair back over her shoulders. "Why would Gus make it up?"

A nervous laugh escaped Heather's mouth. "Just look at the guy. He's . . . no offense . . . a street bum who talks like a Martian. Maybe he's delirious. Maybe he's trying to blackmail the guy. Whatever his deal is, here we are acting like we're the FBI planning our next bust."

"You know, Heather," Jodi said, taking her by the arm and turning her so they were face-to-face, "I agree with you."

They looked at each other for a long second. Heather stopped munching on her gum.

"There's one small thing that makes me think Gus may be at least partially right," Jodi said, letting go of her arm.

"What's that?"

"Faith."

Stan looked up. "She's right, Heather. Faith said that's the place that screwed her up so bad."

"If he's not a legit doctor—," Jodi started to say.

"Yeah, and if they're not real nurses," Stan said.

"Then it's possible they did the procedure on Faith when she may not even have been pregnant," Jodi said, tilting her head.

Stan sighed. "Gosh, I never thought about that."

Heather shrugged. She appeared unconvinced.

"And that's why we've got to at least try to find out if Gus is right," Jodi said. "Either these things are true, or they're not. If this stuff is going on, then everybody who goes in there is at risk."

Heather swatted away a mosquito.

Jodi looked at Heather. "Don't forget, we're talking about big bucks here, too. Gus says Dr. Graham is even bilking the government for services on—"

Heather cut her off. "Gus says this, Gus says that. I'm tired of what that quack says."

Jodi's eyes widened. Stan, too, looked stunned. No one spoke for a minute.

Jodi broke the silence first. She lowered her voice. "Hey, Heather. I didn't ask for this. Gus handed me the letter, remember? Maybe this wasn't an accident. Maybe God wants to use us to help Faith and other people who could be in her same situation."

Heather looked at her feet.

"Look, it's getting late," Jodi said. "Let's just sleep on it, okay? Maybe pray about it, too?"

"I'm done praying," Stan said. "I've just about prayed my eyes out since last week. I'm calling about a job in the morning—"

"You sure, Stan?" Jodi said.

"It's the least I can do for Faith."

Jodi gave him a friendly hug. "Now, whatever you do, don't debate the issue."

"You're the debate queen, remember?" Stan said. "Trust me. I'll stick to football; you can handle the debates."

As they talked, Heather abruptly turned and walked off without saying good-bye.

odi had arrived at work two hours early to get a jump on some research. True, Joey hadn't given her the green light to do the story, but she was on her own time, so she didn't think it would be a problem. She figured she'd start by digging around the back issues of the paper to see if they'd ever done a story on women's clinics in the area.

Unlike the *Philadelphia Inquirer* or the *Los Angeles Times,* both of which had transferred all their articles to a searchable database on the Web, Jodi was stuck plowing through stacks of microfiche copies of the *Montgomery Times.* So far, after thirty tedious minutes with her nose to the microfiche reader, she couldn't find one article.

Jodi's cell phone chirped from inside her purse. She snatched it up on the second ring. "Hi, it's Jodi."

"It's me, Stan," he said just above a whisper.

"Hey, what's up?" She pressed the phone harder against her ear.

"You'll never believe it . . . I just got hired."

Jodi's heart soared. She had a thousand questions but managed to blurt, "Oh my gosh, are you serious? At the clinic?"

"Yeah. But I can't talk right now," Stan said, his voice hoarse.

"It's hard to hear you."

"Sorry, I'm in the lobby on a pay phone and . . . and this place is packed. Have you talked to Heather?"

"No, not yet."

"Listen," Stan said. "If you talk to her, they've got an opening for a phone counselor."

"What about you? What's your job?"

"Stuff . . . I think my thing is called a central supply clerk, but I'm more like a roving gofer—"

"I can't believe this," Jodi said with a wide smile.

"I've really got to go."

"Hey, I'll be praying for you, Stan."

"Thanks, Jodi. Catch you later." He hung up.

Jodi was elated. *Thank you, Lord*, she thought. Last night as she'd drifted off to sleep, she prayed that they'd have a breakthrough or at least some sign that they should move ahead with the "investigation," as Heather had called it, if God wanted her to check out Gus's story.

"Hey, Jodi," her boss called from across the room with a friendly wave. "You're in early today."

Jodi looked up and smiled. This time she actually heard him when he called her name, which was a relief. She'd hate for him to waltz over and see what she was working on. Then again, what was there to hide? She was on her own time. Come to think of it, she thought she'd bring up the story again now that she knew about Faith's situation.

"Hey, got a second?" she said, rising from her chair.

"Let's walk and talk," Joey said, waving her over.

She crossed the room and fell in line behind him as he headed toward Roxanne's office. He looked over his shoulder. "I've got a crazy day. What's up?"

"Um, I know you're opposed to my doing a story on the clinics and . . . on the stuff in that letter—"

He stopped in his tracks and Jodi almost plowed into him.

"Is this about Gus?"

"Well, sort of—" She offered a sheepish smile.

"Then zero."

"—but not totally," Jodi said. "See, it gets kinda complicated. I really, really need to talk to you. Just two minutes, I promise."

"My mind is made up, so talk quick."

She hooked her hair over both ears. "Okay, first of all, I have a friend. She's in the hospital because of a botched job at a clinic."

Joey started to walk again. "I'm listening."

Jodi rushed to catch up. "And, according to Gus—"

"What did I tell you about talking to that man?"

"Okay. Forget him," Jodi said. She took a quick breath. "A source I have says Dr. Victor Graham isn't a licensed doctor . . . and sometimes, according to my source, he performs abortion procedures on people who aren't even pregnant. I believe that might have happened to my friend."

Joey stopped just outside Roxanne's door. A cloud of smoke wafted through the opening. "Rox—got my deposit ready?"

"Almost," Roxanne said, a cigarette fuming between her lips. "Give me a half-second."

"This source," Joey said, turning back to Jodi, his face a picture of skepticism, "does he or she have proof? An eyewitness? Records? Maybe a mole inside the office?"

Jodi wasn't about to mention anything about Stan taking a job at the Total Choice Medi-Center. It was too early for that. While she was sure Stan would be able to find something, at the moment she was empty-handed.

When Jodi didn't immediately respond, Joey continued. "Let me ask you a question. Does your source happen to eat organic mushrooms before gazing into a birdbath, chanting, 'Mirror, Mirror, show me please'?"

"That's not fair, Joey."

"That's what I thought," Joey said, his perfectly white teeth silhouetted behind a full smile. "You don't have a credible source, which means you don't have a story. Not to mention if you're going to make these kinds of accusations, you'd better have at least *two* highly placed, reliable sources . . . Underline the word *reliable*."

"But—"

"Jodi, let's face it. You've got nothing. As I see it, you have a crazy man who feeds the pigeons, and a sick girl with hearsay evidence. Of course I'm sorry about your friend. But that's not good journalism. End . . ."

"I know. End of story," Jodi said, politely finishing his favorite mantra.

"Smart girl." He put a hand on her shoulder. "So, here's what I'd like you to tackle today. I need a 750-word piece on Pennsylvania's outdated voting machines."

"Huh?"

"We're coming up on an election cycle, right?"

"I guess." Jodi was nonplussed. To her, this sounded like a real snoozer assignment.

"And, while it was a hot topic back in Bush versus Gore," Joey said, "nothing's been done to fix the problem. I think readers will be interested in that scoop."

"Here ya go," Roxanne said, interrupting. She handed him a bank bag with a locking, zippered top.

"Kinda light today," Joey said to Roxanne, pretending to weigh the contents in the palm of his hand.

"Not much in the mail this morning," Roxanne said. She returned to her desk and fired up another smoke with the smoldering end of a stub in her ashtray.

He tucked the bag under his arm. "That's just great. I bet Banker Bob will be on my case before noon."

Marge waddled to his side bearing three pink phone messages. Her glasses rested on the end of her nose. "Joey, got three hot ones here." She handed them to him one at a time, rehearsing each message as she did. "That's from your dad . . . said it was urgent and you'd know what it was about."

Joey raised his eyebrows. He took the slip.

"That's about tonight's client meeting. You're to be at Pete's Marina at 5:15. There's a code on there to get through the gate. But he wants you to call him as soon as you can."

Joey studied the message.

Marge took off her glasses. "And that's from Bob Lemstone. He needs to hear from you by lunch."

"What did I tell you," Joey said, looking at the note and then at Jodi. "Banker Bob's lonely. Thanks for making my day, Marge."

"Just doing my job," she said, racing as best she could to answer a phone ringing on her desk.

He looked at Jodi. "So, where were we?"

"Voting machines."

"Right. Have fun with that one, champ." Joey darted for his office.

*Champ?*

She stared at the spot where Joey had stood a moment before. It was bad enough that he didn't seem to care about her story. It was worse to be blown off with such a ridiculous nickname. Sure, she understood Joey's concern about needing credible sources. She agreed and was working on that. Still, although she couldn't pinpoint it, she felt there had to be another reason why Joey opposed her doing the story.

But what?

S tan spent the first two hours of the morning filling out basic employee forms in an unused counseling room. They wanted his Social Security number. Date of birth. Home address. The usual info so Uncle Sam could tax the life out of his wages. He was told to review a thick summary of the Total Choice Medi-Center services as well as a job description.

He was also handed, and was instructed to review, a confidential memo detailing basic "Do's and Don'ts" of his employment. Don't talk to the media. Don't talk to streetside protesters. Don't talk to the clients unless specifically instructed to do so.

Throughout the morning, he felt a mixture of adrenaline and anxiety. He didn't belong here. He wasn't one of them. Surely he'd be found out. He experienced a similar anxiety when Coach Thomas sent him to rival schools during the preseason to size up their offensive strategy—with one giant difference. Here, he was more than an observer. He was part of their team.

Stan felt as if he'd gone over to the dark side.

When he requested permission to call a friend, Jodi's voice was like a breath of fresh air. She was an ally who was praying for him. Still, as he held the phone to his ear, part of his emotions overwhelmed him. He wanted to cry out to the women in the waiting area, "Don't do it!"

At the same time, Stan knew such an outburst would have blown his cover before he learned anything. He was here to help Faith, and he would do the best he could to get Jodi what she needed for her story.

Faith.

As he finished his paperwork, he had plenty of time to think about the fact that she had been here less than two weeks ago. Stan's heart ached at the thought of what she must have felt, coming here behind her dad's back. She had no friends to support her. No one to help her think clearly about her choice. She had to have been so frightened.

And scared.

"All done?" Jenna said, interrupting his thoughts.

"Yes, ma'am."

"Come with me then," she said.

He stood up from the folding chair, thankful to be doing more than sitting alone with his thoughts in the windowless room. Stan handed Jenna the clipboard with his paperwork and followed her out the door.

"Right this way," she said, moving along the six-foot-wide hall. "The doctor would like to have a word with you," she said in a clinical tone.

Stan's heart jumped. He felt like it was the first day of football training camp and he was about to meet the new coach. As he walked, he counted three doors in a row on both sides of the hallway. Each opened to a procedure room. At the end of the hall, they came to a fire door with an oversize sign declaring: STAFF ONLY. Jenna opened it and continued to walk down the hall into the back area. She ushered Stan into the second-to-last room on the right.

"Here we are," she said. "Doctor, this is Stan Taylor."

Dr. Graham looked up from a clipboard of his own with a grunt. He leaned against a counter and made no effort to shake Stan's hand. He wore blue scrubs, and his white face mask hung loosely around his neck. It rested just below his chin. He pointed with the end of his pen to a chair.

"Have a seat." It wasn't a request as much as a command.

Stan sat in the corner.

"You're the new kid Jenna hired today," Dr. Graham said.

"Yes, sir." Stan folded and then unfolded his arms.

"Let me cut to the chase," Dr. Graham said. "Jenna says you've played a little football."

Stan smiled. Here was a topic he felt at home with. "Yes, I've actually got a scholarship to Penn State—"

Dr. Graham waved him off with his pen. "Never mind all of that. My point is, you know how to hustle and how to work as a team, right?"

"Yes, sir," Stan said with a nod, suddenly unsure if he should salute.

"Good. Around here we work as a team. I'm the captain, and what I say goes." Dr. Graham peered at Stan. "Listen. This is a bit unusual. Under normal circumstances, Jenna would give you a more . . . *formal* introduction to your work."

Stan listened, afraid to interrupt the man.

Dr. Graham folded his arms. "You're going to be baptized by fire. Why? We've got a packed house out there, so we've got to stack 'em and move 'em out. Just be glad this isn't Saturday."

Stan gave him a puzzled look.

"That's our busiest day, followed by Friday and then today," Dr. Graham said. "By the weekend, you'll be an old pro . . . if, that is, you can stand the pace."

Jenna stuck her head through the door. She handed him a sheet of paper. "Doctor, we're set and ready when you are."

"Thank you," Dr. Graham said. He studied the page and then turned back to Stan. "As you'll see in a minute, I work fast. Your goal is to keep me from slowing down."

"How's that?"

"By doing exactly what I tell you to do," Dr. Graham said. "Remember, this isn't a beauty parlor. I don't make money having extended conversations with clients. I don't make money holding a patient's hand. And I don't make money answering stupid questions. As long as you focus on my instructions, we'll do fine."

Stan remained silent. More like speechless.

Dr. Graham reached for a box of surgical gloves. "Here's the drill. You probably noticed the six procedure rooms."

"Yes, sir," Stan said, figuring he should say something. "There are three rooms on the left and three on the right of the hall."

If Dr. Graham had heard Stan, he made no sign of it.

"I will be working the left side, and my associate Andrea will work the right." With a snap, Dr. Graham slipped a glove over his left hand and then his right. "I'll run my side of the hall four times in one hour. Andrea isn't quite as proficient as I am—at least not yet."

Stan whistled. He didn't mean to. But the thought that Dr. Graham would do twelve procedures an hour was more than he could imagine. Worse, Stan was still unclear what was expected of him.

"Uh, Dr. Graham—"

"Hold it right there, buster," Dr. Graham said with a snarl like a provoked bear.

"The name's Stan," he said, tired of being treated like a nonperson. The man was a zero in the conversational skills department, and he was starting to look like an even bigger jerk than Stan's own dad.

"Fine . . . Stan." Dr. Graham took a step toward him. "Let me spell it out for you, son. I want no names used. I don't want to know the patient's name—and I sure as blazes don't want them to know mine."

Stan's eyebrows shot up. "So, then, what do I call you?"

"Call me Doc . . . call me sir . . . but don't ever use my name if a patient is around." Dr. Graham wagged a finger as he spoke.

Stan swallowed. "Because?"

"Names are unimportant," Dr. Graham said. "There are a lot of crazies out there. I don't need them bothering me after office hours. Am I clear on this?"

"Yes, sir."

No way would Stan call this man "Doctor" in front of a patient, of that he was sure. How could he? The man was totally unprofessional. In the few minutes Stan had watched him, Dr. Graham failed to show even an ounce of care or compassion for the women he was about to treat.

An iceberg probably gave off more warmth.

Dr. Graham cared for nothing—nothing but hustling through

today's batch. It sickened Stan to think this was the guy who worked on Faith. He watched as Dr. Graham started for the door. "Um, sir? I'm wondering, what is it you want me to do?"

Dr. Graham paused, gripping the doorjamb.

"For the moment, nothing. Today you're on standby. But, for example, if one of my assistants falls behind resetting the rooms for the next patients, I'll need you to give them a hand. Just use the spray bottle to wipe down the surfaces, pull a fresh paper sheet over the table, and make sure there's no blood on the floor."

"I've never—"

"That's immaterial."

"But, I'm not qualified—"

Dr. Graham swore. "You're qualified if I say you're qualified."

Stan took a deep breath. Heather was right. This was nuts. What was he doing here?

Dr. Graham added, "Come to think of it, you'll probably need to give me a hand with the walrus in room 2."

"Excuse me?"

"That cow has already given my staff enough grief. If it comes down to it," Dr. Graham said, "when I call you, all you have to do is hold her steady."

With that, Dr. Graham turned and faced a woman, dressed in scrubs, who appeared at his side. Stan figured she must be Andrea and couldn't help but wonder whether she had any medical training.

"It's showtime," she said, holding up her gloved hands.

"Great," Dr. Graham said. "I've got to get out of here by four, so let's rock'n'roll."

"How about I bet you a bottle of Scotch that I win today?" Andrea said with a smile planted on her face. She turned to leave.

Dr. Graham pulled his mask over his nose. "You're on," he said. He reached forward and gave her a pat on the behind.

As Stan followed the two strangers down the hallway, an over-whelming rush of emotion came over him like a sudden rainstorm.

His throat went dry. His palms grew moist. His breathing started to race. The walls of the hallway closed in. Crushing him. Squeezing the air out of his lungs. His knees started to buckle.

The faces from his nightmare returned. They floated through his mind, their little eyes closed. Round and round they circled. They pointed at him. Accusing him with each revolution.

A line of sweat formed across his forehead, and he wiped it away with the back of his hand and then, for several seconds, braced himself against the wall until he could control his breathing. His chest felt as if it were about to explode.

Several steps ahead, Andrea turned into a room on the right; Dr. Graham turned to the left. Stan could hear but not see Dr. Graham as he approached the first patient.

"Okay, honey buns, do as my assistant told you and this will all be over before you know it."

Stan opened his mouth to shout at the top of his lungs, "He's lying . . . don't believe him . . . It's *never* over . . . It's just beginning. . . . Stop it while you can."

Like a bad dream, the words remained stuck in his throat.

The driver of the Ford Taurus took one last bite from his Wendy's hamburger, crumpled the wrapper, and tossed it into the paper sack. As he did, he noticed a lone French fry in the bottom, fished it out, and then held up the fry as if he had discovered a gold coin.

"One ain't gonna hurt you," he said, holding it out to his partner. "Sure you don't want my last fry?"

"Nah. I've done had about all I can eat," his partner said rolling up the remaining third of his turkey hoagie in its white butcher paper.

Their car idled in the parking lot of WaWa's minimart store across from the Willow Grove Park Mall, a sprawling collection of stores occupying the better part of a hundred acres. From this vantage point, they kept an eye on the bus stop just outside the Kmart. A SEPTA bus was pulling away from the curb, belching a cloud of black diesel exhaust. Three passengers walked toward the bus shelter, which was immersed in fumes.

The driver studied the faces then checked his watch. "Gus is late."

"Roger that."

"Should have been on that bus." The driver tapped a finger against the steering wheel. "Why don't you get your gizmo thingy out and check his location. We don't have all day."

"Sure thing," his partner said, opening the glove compartment. He retrieved the GPS receiver and then fired it up with a push of a button. "So the boss really wants Gus to wear a wire?"

The driver stretched. "Yup. After Gus reported contacting Vic directly last night—"

"Hey, I've been meaning to ask, since when was that the plan?"

"It wasn't. Gus just improvised," the driver said. "Anyway, that kinda forces our hand. The boss says we've got to convince Gus it's time for the next level."

His partner studied the four-inch color screen.

The driver looked over at his associate. "Frankly, there's some concern that Gus might just get whacked . . . before we get what we need on Vic."

He looked up from his screen. "You think the old doctor would actually take Gus out?"

The driver laughed. "In a heartbeat. The doc's as slimy as they come. If Gus really has the goods on him, Vic gets a fresh pair of handcuffs."

"You think it'll matter? Vic got off on appeal last time."

"Trust me, with Gus's info, this time we'll have enough on Vic so he'll spend at least a couple of decades in a federal pen."

"Um, we've got a slight problem," his partner said, studying the screen.

"Don't tell me Gus is still at the hotel? I can hear him now, 'Did you give it . . . to the right people . . . while I overslept—'"

His partner cut off the imitation. "Now that's almost funny," he said. "I wish that were the case." He held out the screen for the driver to see.

"Where's that?"

"Unless it's malfunctioning, according to this, Gus is headed for New York City."

"Impossible, he'd be . . . foolish to leave town now."

"You think he's gonna skip out on us?"

The driver considered that possibility. "No, I don't think so. I'd say he got spooked, but he wouldn't run."

"Then what's he doing?"

"I'd say Gus ditched the tracing bracelet on a train and plans to do this in his own crazy, demented way."

Neither man spoke for a minute.

"I knew seeing Vic was a big mistake on his part," the partner said, watching the developments on his screen.

The driver retrieved his cell phone and started to place a call. As he punched in the numbers, he said, "Whatever Gus is doing, he's on his own. There's no way the department can protect him now."

Jodi sat in her cubicle, scribbling on a yellow legal pad. Voting machines. *Get real,* she thought. Who in the world really cared about all that. Granted, she was raised in a home where her dad always watched the presidential election night returns. She even found herself engaged on some levels, especially as she and her dad discussed the obvious biases of the reporters on the various news channels.

But to think updating voting machines was an issue readers were itching to know about was bogus—at least that was her take. Besides, the next election was almost a year away. There was plenty of time to do a piece on that as it got closer. Still, Joey was the boss, and she would do her best to find out what she could.

Then again, Joey hadn't given her a deadline. He just said to start on it, which she had. She called the League of Women Voters for a statement and almost fell asleep taking notes. She called a manufacturer of the current machines hoping to find someone who could tell her if future modifications were planned, but she gave up after being stuck in their voice mail system for what felt like half the day.

What really kept her going was to picture Stan at the Total Choice Medi-Center. How bizarre to be on the inside. When she threw out the idea last night, she never expected things would move this fast. She was dying to hear from him and couldn't imagine what he was experiencing.

All afternoon she had fought the temptation to call him. She even went so far as to look up the phone number in the yellow pages. She was about to dial but stopped, unsure if employees would be allowed to take personal calls. The last thing she wanted to do was create a problem for Stan on his first day.

She started to doodle. She drew a voter's punch card and then covered it with hanging chads. She scribbled "VOID" across the face of the card.

When the phone in her purse rang, she just about jumped out of her skin. She managed to grab it on the third ring.

"Hello?" She didn't recognize the number appearing in her caller I.D. window.

"Jodi, I'm freaking out over here," Stan said, apparently cupping his mouth with his hand.

"Stan!" She looked up, unsure if she had spoken too loudly. Nobody was looking in her direction. "What's going on?"

"Got a sec?" Stan said just above a whisper.

"Are you kidding? I'm dying for details here. Did you meet him? Did you meet Dr. Graham?"

Stan chuckled. "That guy is one unhappy cockroach."

She felt her heart thumping. "You actually *met* him?"

"I did way more than that, Jodi. And there's so much to tell you," Stan said. "But not now. Like our buddy said, 'There are eyes everywhere' . . . if you know who I mean."

"Gus?"

"Yeah." Stan covered the mouthpiece for a second. She heard muffled sounds in the background and pressed the phone harder against her ear.

"Okay, be right there," she heard Stan say. He started to talk to her again. "Listen, what time do you get off work?"

Jodi glanced at the clock on the wall. "About an hour."

"So do I. Meet me at Johnny Angel's, say, like, 5:15-ish?"

"You're on. Oh, my gosh, Stan, this is so unreal—"

"Hate to cut you off, but they're calling me."

"I'll be there—5:15."

"Oh, one more thing. Got a pencil?"

"Shoot." She flipped to a fresh page in her tablet.

Stan paused. She could hear him rustling a sheet of paper. "Okay, see if you can dig up anything on the Quest Institute of Medicine."

Jodi wrote as fast as her pen would move. "Got it."

"Looks like they give a certificate or whatever for completing a course called 'Practical Nursing.'"

Jodi's mind raced. "Let me guess—you want to find out what it takes to get that certificate, right?"

"Yes, Mom, I'll be home for dinner. I love you," Stan said, a sudden change in his voice.

Jodi heard a click as the connection went dead.

With a push, Stan stuffed another batch of files into the seemingly insatiable paper shredder. He had spent at least fifteen minutes feeding "expiries"—Jenna's word—into its hungry jaws. Jenna had explained that, by law, the clinic was required to keep the confidential client records for two years.

After that, the expiries were reduced to confetti.

That made sense. What else could the clinic do with the mountains of old files? Tossing them in the Dumpster wasn't an option. Jenna claimed antichoice activists would use the information to hound women who thought their decision had been private.

Jenna also ruled out Stan's suggestion of sending the paperwork back to the former patient. She said that would be rude. Stan figured it would remind them of an event they probably were still trying to forget.

Or hide.

From the clinic's perspective, shredding the paperwork was the way to go. Aside from being a bore and a hassle to do, shredding was legal. It was practical.

It was also irreversible.

Curious, Stan stopped the machine. He wanted to see if he could read anything in the wastebasket below. As he sifted through the ultra-thin strips of paper with his fingers, a new idea came to him. He remembered how Faith had said the clinic denied she was ever a patient. Maybe someone standing in this very spot had shredded Faith's file.

No file, no record of her visit.

Maybe that's what happened.

Stan froze.

What if *he* had destroyed her file during the last fifteen minutes?

He kicked himself for being so preoccupied by the events of the day that he hadn't paid attention to what he was shredding. The sudden urge to shut and barricade the door came over him. He needed time to give the seven remaining boxes a careful inspection. If Faith's file was in the stack, he'd have indisputable evidence she could use to sue these jokers.

He stole a glance over his shoulder at the door. He flipped the idea over for a long second. What excuse could he give Jenna for closing and locking the door if she came back to check on him? None came to mind, and he was too mentally wiped out to think straight.

He settled on the idea of paying closer attention to the papers as he worked. He picked up a stack about an inch thick and then scanned through the reports.

Each page told a story. A girl's name, address, and phone number. Her age. Weight. The date of her visit. The estimated age of the fetus. Her vital signs. A series of meaningless codes. And a set of initials from the person who performed the procedure at the bottom of the sheet.

Stan stopped. His forehead wrinkled into a knot. Something wasn't right. He flipped through the information again. Jenna had said they were required to hold the files for two years.

Then it dawned on him.

While most were several years old, he guessed at least a third were dated as recently as a few days ago.

*What's with that?* he thought.

He also noticed that the space where the vital signs—blood pressure, pulse, and temperature—were supposed to be printed had been left blank on many of the forms, both expiries and, especially, the more recent ones.

In a way, it wasn't a surprise. He saw how fast Dr. Graham and Andrea had plowed through the patients all afternoon. Maybe they didn't bother to take the time to fill in the vitals. Maybe it was just an oversight on the part of the medical assistants.

Then again, maybe they never took the vitals in the first place. Stan had no way of knowing for sure. More than ever, he felt like a fish out of water. He wasn't trained in the medical field. He had no idea why vital signs were omitted but instinctively knew that wasn't a good thing.

At the very least, he figured he shouldn't be shredding files that were less than two years old. He'd point the problems out to Jenna.

Without thinking through all the details, a plan emerged. He grabbed a handful of reports and then separated them into two piles. In the first, he stacked files at least two years old. In the second, he put anything that wasn't old enough to be legally destroyed.

He then plucked three reports out of the second pile, each dated as recently as last week. He looked over his shoulder as he folded the three pages and tucked them into the back pocket of his jeans. He faced the wall and began to shred the expiries.

"Here's another box for you," Jenna said.

Stan spun around. His heart thumped against his chest at her sudden entry. Jenna walked through the door holding a brown, two-foot-by-two-foot cardboard container. She placed it on the counter to Stan's right and then rested a hand on top of the box.

"Any questions?" Jenna was professionally dressed, wore white sneakers, her hair pulled back into a ponytail. She was the nicest person Stan had met on the staff. Unlike Dr. Graham, Jenna oozed sincerity. She seemed to really care about the women who came to the Total Choice Medi-Center.

Stan swallowed.

He wondered if his face appeared as guilty as he felt. The three pages tucked in his back pocket seemed to burn a hole through his pants. He was positive she could hear the mad pounding of his heart. For a quick second, he studied her expression but, thankfully, didn't detect any suspicion.

"Actually, yes," Stan said, his mind now racing faster than his heart.

He gazed at Jenna's name tag, stalling for time as he labored to frame the right question. Where was Jodi when he needed her?

"Yes?" Jenna's face, like the Mona Lisa, was pleasant. And yet Stan could somehow tell she didn't have much time.

Stan punted. He decided to take the indirect approach. "Look, um, Jenna, I'm just curious. How did you decide to work at a . . . a clinic like this?"

Her lips eased into a warm smile. "You know, Stan, that's a great question. I guess I've always been interested in women's rights and all that. Back in high school, I knew one day I would get involved in women's issues, maybe as a counselor. As it turned out, I landed here."

Stan fed another file into Mr. Shreds, trying to appear busy. He nodded. He hoped the pages in his back pocket didn't decide to leap out and point a finger at him.

Jenna rested a hip against the edge of the table. "I see what we do as an opportunity to help girls . . . and women of all ages . . . make it through what is a tough time in their lives. We really do get them through their personal crises. I like that about my job."

Stan pictured Faith lying in a hospital bed, her face pale. Talk about a crisis. He wondered what Jenna would say about helping Faith through the loss of their home and her inability to have kids in the future, all because she had come to this place.

"Uh, well, I do have, like, a question about these," Stan said. He reached for the second stack of reports and then handed them to Jenna.

Jenna held them but didn't look at them for more than two seconds. "Is there something wrong?"

"Well," Stan said, keeping his tone even, "I happened to notice these, um, files aren't at least two years old. I wasn't sure if I should be shredding them."

Jenna's face reddened. She leafed through the pages, looked up, and, as her body stiffened, handed them back. "You read these?"

He shrugged. "The dates, mostly."

"Stan, frankly, what's in these files is none of your business. They're confidential—or were."

Stan was taken aback by her sudden coolness.

"If Dr. Graham said they're ready for disposal, then it's not my place—or yours—to question him."

Up until a minute ago, he didn't think she was the type that would swat a fly. Now he wasn't so sure. So much for her Mona Lisa smile.

"Jenna, I'm sorry. I wasn't, like, questioning the doctor. I just wanted to make sure it wasn't an honest mistake, um, seeing how busy we all are." He offered a smile.

Jenna softened. "I appreciate that, Stan. Just stick to the job and trust Dr. Graham's judgment." She returned Stan's smile. "Now, if you'll excuse me." She turned and left the room.

Stan stared at the files in his hand for a long minute.

Fine. Whatever.

He dumped them through the shredder, reached for another handful, stuffed them into the machine. He'd do his job, but trust Dr. Graham's judgment? Trust a man who didn't even want his patients to know his name? Trust a guy who injured Faith and then denied any wrongdoing?

*Right,* Stan thought, finishing off the last of the two stacks. He was boiling mad as he retrieved the box Jenna had just delivered. He removed the lid and grabbed another handful.

Stan was about to shove the first few pages into the shredder when he stopped dead in his tracks. Something on the top of the first file screamed for attention. With a squint, he focused on the personal data section. He felt his lungs almost collapse as he read the patient's name.

Faith Morton.

ᔐ

For Jodi, any hope of working on the voting-machine story flew out the window with Stan's call. A hundred questions, no, double that, poured into her mind, not the least of which was: How in the world did he manage to get the job?

True, Stan was a charmer when he wanted to be, as anyone at school could atest. But Stan had a better chance of being struck by lightning than landing a position in a clinic—at least that had been Jodi's view before his call.

To think Stan actually met Dr. Graham. How unreal.

What did he look like? Talk like? Act like?

Was Gus right about Dr. Graham? Did he really race with another "doctor" to see who could do the most procedures? Had he surrounded himself with inexperienced workers, handpicked and personally trained? Come to think of it, Stan didn't have any qualifications, so what had he been doing all day?

More important, she wondered what Stan was feeling. He had been such a mess last night. And, given what he had said about Faith being in the hospital, he had to be struggling to keep himself together emotionally.

She knew the answers would have to wait until she and Stan touched base at Johnny Angel's. She checked her watch. Time seemed to inch forward slower than a snail's pace in winter. At least she, scouring the Web, had managed to dig up some very interesting background on the Quest Institute of Medicine.

She was itching to tell Stan that, for starters, the "institute" only offered correspondence courses over the Internet. She noticed a disclaimer in very fine print, which stated the institute was both "unaccredited by and unaffiliated with the National Medical Board Association."

*Big surprise there,* she thought. Not to mention that the syllabus describing the "Practical Nursing" class looked like a total fluff course, on par with basket weaving for beginners.

But the most telling detail was the address of the Quest Institute. Jodi's first suspicions were aroused when she noticed the institute was located in Pennsylvania. On a hunch, she used the MapQuest feature on the Web and typed in the street info.

Voilà! It was what she had guessed.

The location of the Quest Institute of Medicine shared the parking lot with the Total Choice Medi-Center. How convenient for Dr. Graham.

Of course, she didn't have any proof that the two were somehow connected—at least not yet. She was working on that angle when her cell rang.

"Hi, it's Jodi."

"Hey, Mom?"

Jodi's face broke into a wide smile. "What's up, Stan?"

"Listen, Mom, I'm gonna be a little late for dinner, okay?"

"Stan, what in the world—"

"I'm sorry, but it's probably more like seven."

That Stan wasn't able to talk was clear. Why? Again, she'd have to wait even longer to find out. She felt silly but decided to play along. "Yes, dear, seven will be fine."

"I love you, Mom."

"I love—" Jodi stopped herself. She raised half an eyebrow and lowered her voice. "Stan, is this one of your tricks to get me to say, 'I love you'?"

She heard him laugh and then say, "Big kisses, too."

*Boy, he's really milking this,* she thought. Still, an image of she and Stan sharing a dance under very unusual circumstances several weeks ago came to mind.

She didn't have feelings for him . . . did she?

She'd never considered Stan an option before he got saved. She was well aware of the places in the Bible that warned against becoming joined together with someone who didn't share a faith in Jesus. Now that Stan was a believer, everything had changed. Right?

Jodi swallowed.

Feeling slightly lightheaded, her face suddenly flushed with warmth. She toyed with the implications of this new thought. If—and it was a big *if*—she and Stan started to date, she'd have to face the fact that such a move would doom her relationship with her best friend, Heather.

Heather, after all, thought Stan hung the moon.

Jodi twirled several strands of hair. What kind of a crazy idea was this? As if Stan "da Man" and she would ever be an item. She put the cell phone back into her purse, paused, and then retrieved her compact to check her makeup.

*You just never know,* she thought.

T he sixty-five-foot Viking Sport Cruiser towered a proud four-teen feet above the water line. Its sleek profile projected the sensation of speeding through the water even though it remained tethered at Pete's Marina. The yacht, gassed with 960 gallons of fuel, could easily cruise the Delaware River, out into the Atlantic Ocean, and be dockside by eleven o'clock without breaking a sweat.

On the main deck Dr. Graham and Joey Stephano sat in the captain's chairs at the two-person helm, beverages in hand. Dr. Graham had just finished giving Joey the grand tour, and he knew, by the wide-eyed look still plastered on Joey's face, that the man was impressed.

Joey had seemed like a kid on Christmas morning when Dr. Graham demonstrated the set of remote-controlled panels that concealed two garages under the port and starboard sunpads. An unused, brand-new, high-performance Jet Ski was parked in bay one. The other bay was home to an inflatable dinghy pleasure craft with outboard motor.

Dr. Graham had taken Joey down the six steps that led to the lower deck. There the master stateroom, on the port side aft, awaited. Its angled king berth, heated towel racks, and private bath were fit for a king. The VIP port guest stateroom with queen-size bed was equally luxurious.

He had found Joey's gasps amusing as they toured the salon with its U-shaped, leather bench sofa and highly polished dinette. The space was bathed in soft, indirect lighting. The fully equipped galley with island wet bar was draped in an elegant blend of cherry and mahogany wood paneling. The floor, covered in an off-white, thick berber carpet, was accented with chrome trim.

Even now, two hired catering attendants buzzed between the main and lower decks. They served appetizers, topped off drinks, and prepared to grill shrimp and steak on the integrated electric grill adjacent to the aft swim platform.

The sun, now a red fireball, hovered just above the Philadelphia skyline in the hazy horizon. It cast a splash of color across the surface of the Delaware River. The winds were low, the water calm. The night was off to a good start, with one exception.

Jenna.

Dr. Graham checked his watch, annoyed and concerned that Jenna was almost twenty minutes late. She was as punctual as anyone he'd ever worked with. *What's keeping her?* he thought.

"Please forgive me, but I've got to ask," Joey said, swirling his glass of white wine.

"Shoot."

"What's something like this go for these days?"

"You in the market?" Dr. Graham said, raising an eyebrow.

Joey smiled. "Never mind. It was probably rude of me to ask. Something like this is way out of my league."

"Maybe, maybe not," Dr. Graham said. "One-point-eight, to answer your question."

Joey almost choked. "As in million?"

Dr. Graham tilted his glass as if to say, "Yes."

He studied Joey with an amused interest. Joey, dressed in his khakis and navy blue and white Hawaiian shirt, was not what he would have pictured as a newspaperman. True, he had told Joey to come casual. Still, Dr. Graham had expected somebody a little less *GQ*-looking.

In any case, Joey had a refreshingly unstuffy appeal. Even though they had spent less than an hour together, Dr. Graham was already convinced they could do business.

Lots of business.

An attendant holding a tray approached and inquired about their drinks.

Joey placed his unfinished glass of wine on the tray and said, "Maybe I will have that beer after all."

Dr. Graham tapped the rim of his glass indicating more of the same and then dismissed the waiter with a nod.

"As soon as Jenna gets here," Dr. Graham said, "I thought we'd cruise up the Delaware and gawk at the fat-cat mansions just north of Riverside, New Jersey."

Joey relaxed against the back of his chair, his arms dangling at its sides. "This is all very nice of you. Can't say I've ever had this kind of red-carpet treatment from any of the other advertisers with our paper."

Dr. Graham took it as a compliment but sensed a slight hesitation in Joey's voice.

"Blame it on this," Joey said, tapping the side of his nose, "but the reporter in me wonders if there's somehow a catch."

"That's what I like," Dr. Graham said, "a man who isn't afraid to speak his mind. And, while we all have to make our little compromises along the way, don't worry. There's no catch. There's just this." He reached into a pocket, withdrew a thick manila envelope, and then tossed it into Joey's lap.

Joey picked it up. "What's this, my friend?"

Dr. Graham leaned forward. "That's $5,000—cash."

Joey looked around as if he were in the middle of a drug deal. He peeled open the flap and peeked in. A banded wad of $100 bills was stuffed inside. He brought the money to his nose, as if smelling it would somehow assure him this wasn't a dream.

Dr. Graham sipped his drink. He winked. "Consider it a bonus or, if you like, a goodwill gesture."

Joey pointed to himself. "You think I need this?"

"I *know* you need it," he said. "And, in case you're wondering, our agreement stands. We agreed to a referral fee of $25 for every customer who answers our ad running in your paper. Naturally, my office will send a check for that total each week. Let's just say that this, however, is an added token of my appreciation for the opportunity to work with such a fine young man."

A fresh round of drinks arrived.

"And another thing," said Dr. Graham as he took a beverage from the waiter's tray. "I understand your paper has experienced the same rodent infestation we have."

Joey met his gaze with a blank stare.

"I'm not sure I know—"

"Oh, I believe you do."

Dr. Graham paused for effect. "He's been spreading around his slanderous venom, gross misrepresentations, and flagrant lies with his little white envelopes."

Joey nodded. "Now that you mention it, I know the pest."

"Then, as you know, such vermin will spread their diseased ideas unless they're properly mitigated," Dr. Graham said, offering a single wink in his left eye. "Like cancer, it's always best to stop it in the early stages."

Joey swallowed. "There's nothing like a good ending to a bad story—as it were."

"I agree." Dr. Graham raised his glass to make a toast. "By midnight tomorrow, your rodent population will be greatly reduced."

Joey raised his glass.

"And, here's to many future . . . bonuses."

⮂

A woman stood at the gate to Pete's Marina, camera in hand. She rested her left elbow on top of a three-foot brick wall to balance the Nikon F-15 and its bulky 300x telephoto zoom lens in the palm of her left hand. With her right hand she manually focused the lens until the two men on the boat were crystal-clear.

The rapid-fire, auto-advance feature whirled as she pressed the shutter release with her right forefinger.

*Click. Click. Click. Click. Click.*

She looked up from the viewfinder, adjusted the angle of her position, and then pressed her eye to the camera. She zeroed in on the man on the left. He held a tan envelope.

*Click. Click. Click. Click.*

tan's heart was about to explode. The instant he left the Total Choice Medi-Center, he hustled over to Kinko's and made copies of Faith's chart. Standing over the copy machine, he had half expected someone to burst through the double glass doors and haul him off to jail for snatching the confidential information.

As if the fear of getting busted wasn't enough of a heartstopper, he decided to go directly to Pastor Morton. Even though the man had flipped out at him in the hospital, this time Stan was bringing good news. That should count for something, he figured. Armed with a copy of Faith's file, Pastor Morton should be able to at least get the clinic to pay Faith's hospital expenses.

Stan pulled into view of the Mortons' house, a one-story, light blue cottage framed by a front porch. The steepled roof over the porch was supported by four white pillars. Stan, embarrassed by the way he had taken advantage of Faith, almost couldn't bring himself to look at the bench swing mounted on the right side of the porch.

He rolled his car to a stop by the curb. An internal alarm in the front of his brain went haywire. It screamed, "Do Not Enter!" as if he were about to enter a biohazard area.

Pastor Morton, hammer in hand, was bent over a sign that read, "For Sale by Owner." With a final series of swings, he pounded it into the freshly cut, pint-size yard. His white T-shirt was soaked through in spots. He wore an old fishing hat; his sneakers were caked with grass trimmings. A lawn mower, an edger, and a gas can sat on the sidewalk.

Stan guessed Pastor Morton was done for the day, which was a plus. At least he hadn't arrived while Faith's dad was busy.

He cut off the engine, grabbed a copy of Faith's file, and then stepped out of the car.

"She's not here," Pastor Morton said, annoyed. He straightened up to his full height in a slow, unhurried movement. His fingers gripped the hammer so tight his knuckles whitened. "I would prefer that you weren't, either."

Stan took a deep breath. He wasn't about to let this man get the better of him. "Wow, she's still in the hospital?"

"What if she is?" Pastor Morton said, wiping the sweat from his brow with the bottom of his shirt. "This is none of your business, Stan Taylor."

Stan took a baby step forward onto the sidewalk. He put his hand in his left front pocket and then tucked the file under his arm. "I tried to call—"

"It's disconnected."

"I know; that's why I came, Pastor," Stan said, inching forward.

"Son, maybe your head has been banged around too many times on that football field. So I'll say this once again and pray that it will register this time." He raised the hammer and pointed with it to the street. "I want you to get off my property. Stay away from Faith. And stay out of our lives." He whirled around and stomped toward the house.

Even though his words stung, Stan left the safety of the sidewalk and took two steps into the yard. "Hey, Pastor. Doesn't the Bible say something like, um, 'Forgive one another'?"

Pastor Morton stopped on the second step with one foot resting on the deck. He didn't turn to face Stan. "I have forgiven you. But if you're looking for a happy Kodak moment, you've come to the wrong place. Now, leave me be."

With that, Pastor Morton crossed the short distance to the screen door, opened it, stepped inside, and allowed the screen door to hit the jamb with a bang behind him.

Frustrated, Stan turned back toward his car. What was the point of trying to talk to that guy? Here he had good news but wasn't even given the chance to share it. Not to mention that he had taken a huge risk when he smuggled Faith's file out of the clinic.

Stan climbed behind the wheel of his car. If Pastor Morton wanted him to leave, then fine. That's exactly what he'd do. Let him miss out on the good news he was bringing. Why bother with the old crab? As if in answer to his question, one word popped into his mind.

*Grace.*

Stan remembered talking about grace with Jodi and Heather last night over pizza. Jodi said grace was a gift. She said grace was something we didn't deserve and something we couldn't earn. Stan was about to start the car when a voice somewhere in the back of his mind prompted him to consider what grace looked like in this situation.

After all, as a football player, he didn't usually think in terms of grace. The opponents always got what was coming to them. Like they say, fight fire with fire. Naturally, the whole concept of grace was foreign to him. And yet he had experienced God's grace several weeks ago when he gave his heart to Christ.

Stan thought, *So, God, you want me to suck it up and march in there anyway and give this to him—is that it?* Stan clenched his teeth for a long minute. His head fell back against the headrest. In the silence that followed, a peaceful sensation eased over him like a spring breeze. *Okay, here goes nothing,* he thought as he got out of the car. He walked to the house, stepped onto the porch's gray floorboards and moved to the screen door.

With a tap on the frame, he said, "Pastor Morton?" He squinted through the screen door and saw Pastor Morton through the mesh. He sat in the shadows with a glass of water and a towel over his shoulder but didn't answer. He wiped his head with the towel.

"Look, Pastor," Stan said, talking through the screen. "I came because I have some seriously great news. I just need a minute."

Pastor Morton drank the rest of his water and placed the glass on the floor between his feet. He cleared his throat. "Whatever you're selling, I'm not interested." He waved Stan off, leaned forward, resting his elbows on his knees, and then buried his face in his hands.

On impulse, Stan opened the screen door and stepped inside. He knew he was probably pushing it, but he also remembered something he and Jodi had read in the Bible. Jesus had challenged his disciples by saying, "Blessed are the peacemakers." Although he was a young believer, he still felt as if he should try out the peacemaker role, especially in this situation.

Stan sat on the edge of the well-worn brown sofa positioned under the front window. He placed the file on the coffee table between them. As he settled in, he almost blurted out, "I come in peace," but decided it sounded too much like Buzz Lightyear.

Stan rubbed his hands together and cracked his knuckles just as his coach had done on many occasions in the locker room before delivering a pep talk. "Okay. Um, please, hear me out. I know this is gonna sound crazy, but I got this from the clinic where"—Stan suppressed a cough—"where Faith got messed up."

Pastor Morton looked up. His face drained of what little color he had. "I'm in no mood for your crazy talk. If this is one of your pranks—"

Stan shook his head. "I promise you, it's not. If you don't believe me, look at this." Stan pushed the file across the coffee table.

"Why should I?" he said, dabbing the towel around the base of his neck. "Like I said, I'm not interested."

Stan felt like jumping across the coffee table to shove the papers in his face. "Sir, that's Faith's file . . . from the clinic."

Pastor Morton stared, his face a mixture of disbelief and amazement. "That's impossible. They denied—"

"I know."

Pastor Morton leaned forward in his chair. He carefully picked up and cradled the paperwork in his hands as if he had been handed a newborn. He reached and gathered his reading glasses from the end table, put them on, and started to pore over the information. After a full three minutes, he said, "I don't understand. Where did you get this? You know someone who works at this place?"

Stan nodded. "Well, sort of. It's kind of a long story. Today was my first day."

Pastor Morton stared over the edge of his glasses. He motioned with a hand for Stan to continue.

"See, my friend Jodi works at a local newspaper," Stan said, rolling his head around his neck. "She had been working on a story about clinics . . . like this place. She got a tip that some pretty far-out things were going on. So she suggested that maybe I get a job to see for myself."

"You steal this?"

Stan scrunched his nose. "Well, sir, not really. It was about to be tossed into a shredder. I'd say it was one of those God things where I happened to be in the right place at the right time, you know?"

Pastor Morton looked back at the pages.

Stan said, "I figured they either made a mistake by tossing this out, or—"

"Or they were covering up their tracks. Is that what you think?"

Stan shrugged. "Yeah, looks that way. The main thing is, you and Faith have proof she was there when . . . when she got, you know." Stan swallowed as he stood to leave. "Anyway, I hope this helps, and I really am, um, sorry about what you and Faith are going through . . . because of me."

Pastor Morton pointed to the bottom corner of the page. "Do you know whose initials these are?"

"Dr. Victor Graham's," Stan said. He started for the door.

Pastor Morton rose from his chair and crossed the room to the front door. "Do me one favor, will you?"

Stan looked down. He thought he knew what was coming. He was sure Pastor Morton was going to remind him to stay away from Faith. "What's that?"

Pastor Morton put a hand on Stan's shoulder and gave it a surprisingly firm squeeze. "I was wrong to take out my anger on you. Will you forgive me for coming down on you so hard?"

Surprised, Stan looked up and offered him a quick smile. "Yeah, sure thing."

Pastor Morton kept his grip on Stan's shoulder. "See, I guess I've been mad at you because, well, if my daughter were to die because of this . . . ," he said, swallowing hard. "What I'm trying to say is that . . . Faith is not ready—"

"How's that?"

Pastor Morton released his hand. "I'm embarrassed to say this, Stan, but I'm a preacher and my own daughter doesn't share my faith in God."

*No wonder,* Stan thought. It wasn't just the fact that Faith had embarrassed her dad by sleeping with a jock like him—as wrong as that had been. What could be worse than to think your kid might die without believing in Jesus?

This time, Stan reached out and squeezed Pastor Morton's shoulder. "You know what? I'm gonna pray that God answers your prayers for Faith."

"Thank you, Stan."

Stan stepped through the doorway and then, standing on the front porch, turned around. "There's something else . . . and it's kind of a biggy."

"What's that, son?" Pastor Morton said, his glasses resting on the end of his nose.

"I'm no expert, but if I read that chart right," Stan said with a nod in the direction of the papers, "Faith wasn't even pregnant."

Women's Services," said the voice on the other end of the phone. "This is Delores."

"Excuse me, but is this the Total Choice Medi-Center?" Jodi asked, rechecking the number she had dialed. She figured she'd do a little investigative reporting since Stan was running late.

"Yes. How can I serve you?" said Delores, her voice warm and inviting.

"Um, I think I may be pregnant," Jodi said, knowing full well since she was a virgin that would be impossible. "Gosh, my dad will, like, kill me if he finds out I'm . . . you know." She pretended to sound nervous and hoped she wasn't overdoing the drama.

"I'm so glad you called," Delores said. "This is a very personal decision, and I'm here to help. Would you mind telling me your first name?"

Jodi bit the end of her pen and then decided to jump in with both feet. "It's Jodi—but, um, do you have to tell my parents?"

"Relax, Jodi. We're just talking right now, okay? Everything will be fine," Delores said, speaking the words with a smooth, soft tone. "But first, let's start with a simple question. When was the date of your last period?"

Jodi had anticipated this. She gave a date.

Delores said, "Okay. Just give me a second while I figure this up."

Jodi said, "I know I can be somewhat irregular, but I don't ever remember it being this late."

"Of course, Jodi. I understand. Looks like it's been ten weeks."

Jodi blew a long breath. "Gosh."

"There's no reason to be alarmed, Jodi," Delores said. "Tell me, Jodi, how old are you?"

"Um, sixteen. But I'll be seventeen in a couple of days."

"Then let me be the first to say happy birthday."

Jodi switched the phone to her other ear. "Thanks, um, Delores. I guess this is one present I, like, wasn't looking for."

"Jodi, remember, we're here for you," Delores said. "We can take care of the problem if you'd like."

"I . . . I just don't know where to turn," Jodi said.

Delores said, "You know, Jodi, we've been caring for women for many years. You'll see we have a great team that can walk you through this. It really can be all over before you know it."

"Really? What about telling my parents?"

"No one needs to know." Delores added, "Before we hang up, I'll provide you with a phone number to call. Just listen to the prerecorded message that describes the choice you're about to make. I know it's a hassle, but it's one of those government regulations we've got to comply with."

"Like, when should I call?"

"Tonight is best. That way you'll have satisfied the waiting period requirement, at least as far as we're concerned. It's really that simple. Like I said, no one needs to know."

That didn't sound right to Jodi. She knew Pennsylvania had a parental-consent law on the books. She had even debated the informed-consent issue with other students in social studies class. Maybe Gus was right. He claimed that the clinic would just tell her to use a different color pen while forging her parent's signature on the consent form.

Delores interrupted her thoughts. "Tell me, Jodi, have you ever been pregnant?"

"No. And we, that is, this guy from school and I, only did it once. I thought he loved me. I thought he was the one. But now, after I, like, told him the bad news, he doesn't want anything to do with me."

"Jodi, I'm sure you know that once is all it takes. And you acted on what you thought at the time. Don't get down on yourself. We all make mistakes, and an unwanted pregnancy doesn't have to be a scary thing," Delores said. "The way I see it, you're so young. You have your future ahead of you. Let me guess—you probably have plans to go to college and get married one day, right?"

"Yeah, that would be nice."

"And you're probably thinking that having a baby now would get in the way of all that."

"Uh-huh."

"Do you know what, Jodi? I talk with women every day who are in the same situation as you are," Delores said. "They feel trapped. Is that how you feel?"

"Wow, how did you know?"

Delores seemed amused by the question. "Oh, probably because I assist women just like you every day."

"But, is it, um, expensive?" Jodi tapped the end of her pen against the edge of the desk.

"First, let me say I believe you would be making the best decision of your life."

"Really?"

"Absolutely. This way, you'll be able to finish high school without the stigma and hassles of being pregnant." Delores cleared her throat. "And, beyond that, this choice will allow you to chase your dreams."

"I . . . I never thought of it like that," Jodi said. She was amazed at how polished Delores was sounding. She'd make an awesome used-car salesman.

"You asked about the money. Right now, we can make this problem disappear for $295. That includes an on-site pregnancy test and pelvic exam to verify your status. Would you like for me to arrange an appointment?"

"Oh, gee, I don't think I can afford—"

"What about savings?"

Jodi offered a nervous laugh. "Can't say I've started a savings account yet."

Delores said, "What about your friends? Could you borrow it? You know, get five dollars, ten dollars, or whatever they have. You can always get a job and pay them back."

"Yeah, I guess . . . ," Jodi said, pretending to be discouraged.

"I'll tell you what," Delores said. "The longer you put off this procedure, the more expensive it will become, and we wouldn't want that now, would we?"

Jodi remained quiet.

Delores said, "Jodi, come see me tomorrow with whatever you can afford, and we'll see what we can do for you, okay?"

Jodi hesitated then said, "All right."

"Be sure to ask for me, Delores. I'll be in the reception area, and I'll make sure you get the royal treatment."

Jodi thought, but didn't say, *Yeah, and a commission for reeling me in.* Instead, she decided to explore a different avenue.

"Oh, I was wondering something else, Delores."

"Yes, Jodi?"

"Um, like, is the person who does this procedure a doctor? I mean, not to be overly cautious . . . but you hear stories in the news and such."

Delores paused, then said, "Let me assure you, Jodi, our clinic is a first-class facility. We employ only the highest-qualified people in the field and have thousands of satisfied customers. You'll be in good hands."

Jodi noticed Delores didn't answer the question. How difficult would it have been for her to say, "Yes, Dr. So-and-So is board-certified by the National Medical blah blah blah"?

Jodi tried another angle. "That's good, but, um, I have another question if that's okay."

"Of course, Jodi. Although we close for the day in a few minutes, I'm here for you."

"Okay, great." Jodi took a quick breath. "Well, see, I've heard

about—complications, or whatever—like getting a punctured uterus . . .
excessive hemorrhaging . . . and stuff like that. Anyway, so I'm kinda
wondering how often that happens at, um, your clinic." Jodi bit her lip.
She added, "You know, I just want to be on the safe side if I go through
with all this."

Again, Delores seemed to pause longer, as if trying to choose her
words carefully.

"Jodi, believe me when I say it's natural to wonder about these
matters. I understand how you feel, too. I'd probably be asking many
of the same questions. But there comes a time when you have to
decide for yourself if this choice is right for you."

*Are you going to answer my question?* Jodi thought.

Delores said, "I'll tell you what, Jodi. Come in tomorrow and bring
any questions you may have. I'm confident our staff and our facility
will put your mind at ease. When can I expect you?"

"Uh, what time do you open?"

"Nine o'clock," Delores said. "You'll be back on your feet before
noon with a smile on your face. I promise."

"Wow. Really?" Jodi said, the palms of her hands moist with fear
at the prospect of carrying the charade that far. "Guess I'll see you at
nine."

"That's a good girl," Delores said. "And don't forget your money."

"Bye." Jodi lowered the phone into the cradle. She sat motionless,
too deep in thought to move. Delores was good. Really good. She
appeared to care. And, for all Jodi knew, maybe she did care. Before
making the call, Jodi would have viewed Delores as just some glorified
telemarketer, anxious to make a quick sale at Jodi's expense.

Now she wasn't so sure.

On the other hand, if Delores cared about her crisis as much as
she appeared to, Jodi wondered why she dodged her questions about the
physical risks. Come to think of it, why didn't she present any of the
other choices? Delores didn't mention giving up the baby for adoption.
She didn't really explore the idea of Jodi marrying her "boyfriend."

How ironic. With a name like Total Choice Medi-Center, you'd think they'd offer a range of options. *Maybe a better name would have been the* Only *Choice Medi-Center,* she thought, suppressing a smile.

Still, the most troubling part of the conversation was how convincing Delores appeared to be. Jodi wondered what she would have honestly done had she *really* been in a crisis. After all, in less than ten minutes, Delores felt like a friend.

A trustworthy adviser.

An ally.

In the quiet of the moment, it dawned on her that she would have made a lifelong decision based on nothing more than the assurances of a complete stranger.

Just as Faith had done.

A trip to Johnny Angel's, the local favorite burger-and-shake hangout, was like a trip back in time. Sporting a fifties retro décor, posters of Chuck Berry, Dion and the Belmonts, and Bill Haley and the Comets were mounted on the walls. A life-size Elvis cardboard figurine was propped in a corner near the giant jukebox.

Black and white floor tiles were arranged like a giant checkerboard, and a row of red vinyl bar stools were parked at an ice cream bar where waitresses, dressed as if at a sock hop, served generous scoops of hand-dipped treats into tall Coca-Cola glasses.

Stan and Jodi sat across from each other in a booth in the back corner. Stan had ordered a root beer float; Jodi, a strawberry shake. She kept reminding herself this wasn't exactly a date. They were here "on business." Just the same, every so often she'd look up from her shake and catch Stan looking at her, or so she thought.

The jukebox finished playing "Teen Angel" and then launched into "Love Potion #9." Stan leaned back against the wall, stretching his legs across his side of the booth. He drained the rest of his float and then licked the end of the straw.

"So, I have to know," Jodi said. "How in the world did you find Faith's file?"

"Like you say, 'It's a God thing,'" Stan said, setting down the cup. "It just kind of dropped in my lap. Oh, and I have three other files I need to give you."

She raised an eyebrow. "Why's that?"

"I dunno. Maybe you can use them as evidence for your story," he said. "Let's just say Dr. Graham wanted me to shred a whole bunch of files we're supposed to keep."

"Gosh, I still can't believe you actually met the guy."

"Jodi, I've never done anything so wild in my life."

Jodi wiped her mouth with a napkin. Her cell phone rang in her purse. She pulled it out, glanced at the caller I.D., and then silenced the ring without answering. "Sorry. So, it was really nuts, huh?"

"Like you wouldn't believe. I mean," Stan said, "get this. On my first day, Dr. Graham had me hauling these bottles, or whatever, with the remains from the, uh, procedures to the back room where some guy strains out the blood—"

"Um, Stan, we're eating—"

"Before putting the baby back together . . . just to make sure all the parts are there, you know, so nothing is left inside the patient—"

"Stan—"

"And then he grinds them up in the sink disposal—"

Jodi reached across the table and pinched his arm.

"Ouch! Why'd you do that?"

"I get the picture," Jodi said, her eyes wide as saucers.

Stan rubbed his arm. "Yeah, well, maybe . . . but I doubt it."

She folded her arms. "What does that mean?"

"Only that unless you see it for yourself, you have no idea what's going on back there," Stan said. He leaned his head against the wall and closed his eyes. "To see all those little babies lined up waiting to be tossed down the sink . . . it's worse than going to a . . . a horror movie. I'm telling you, I'll never forget it."

She uncrossed her arms. "Okay, so you're right. I don't know what you're talking about. It's, like, hard to imagine that goes on all the time. But guess what?"

He looked over at her.

"I've got an appointment to see Delores at the clinic in the morning. I told her I thought I was pregnant."

"Wow. So you're really gonna see if Gus is right?"

Jodi nodded. "Yeah. Joey says I need to have, like, at least two credible witnesses for a story. I figure there's you . . . and now there's me. You know, teamwork and all that." Her face flushed, hoping he wouldn't read too much into her comment.

He smiled. "I'll be sure to wave."

"Actually, if you do, you'll blow my cover and I'll probably claw out both your eyes," she said. "Seriously, Stan. Don't get me in trouble. I'm already taking a big risk here."

"Hey, you know me—"

"Exactly. That's the problem," she said. "But there *is* something I need from you."

"Sure. Like what?" Stan said, bringing a finger to his forehead as if deep in thought. "Let me guess—you need a kiss?"

Jodi blushed. "Yeah, and then maybe you'd turn back into a toad."

Stan slammed his hand to his chest as if stabbed with a dagger. "Arrgh. You sure know how to hurt a guy."

Jodi hooked her hair over her right ear. "You'll survive. Anyway, if I'm gonna do this, I need you to, um, provide a urine sample."

Stan smirked.

"What's so funny?"

He reached into his pocket. "Gotcha covered. One donation coming right up." He placed a two-inch plastic cup with a white lid and a Total Choice Medi-Center label on the table. Pushing it toward her, Stan said, "Somehow I just knew you'd be doing something crazy like this."

ᔕ

"Hey there," Jodi said, plopping down on the sofa next to her mom. She pulled her hair back and, with a scrunchy, formed a ponytail.

"Hey, honey. You're home kinda late. How was your day?" Rebecca Adams said, turning a page in the Talbot's summer catalog.

Jodi sighed. "Beyond crazy."

"You wanna talk about it?"

"Yeah, but maybe later, Mom. Where's Dad?"

"Out back, I think."

"Cool. Any messages?"

"Heather called. She's at home. I'd say she sounded upset. You guys have a fight?"

"Not that I know of . . . but, like, when did she call?"

"I'd say around seven."

Jodi had been meaning to call Heather all day, especially since she'd stormed off without saying good night. Jodi looked at her watch. Almost nine. *Heather's steaming by now,* she thought. Jodi kissed her mom on the side of the head and stood to leave. "I'd better call and see what's up."

"There's leftovers in the fridge—"

"Thanks, Mom," Jodi said from the hallway. She grabbed the kitchen cordless, a bottle of water, and then dialed.

"Hey, it's me," Jodi said, the phone wedged between her ear and shoulder.

"It's about time you called. Where have you been?" Heather seemed to spit out the words.

"Um, at work." Jodi took a drink of water.

"After that I mean. I even tried your cell phone."

"Heather, like, what's with the interrogation?"

No answer.

"Is this about Stan?" Jodi said. "Let me guess—you're jealous because of his attention to Faith, is that it?"

"No."

"Then what's this about?"

"You."

"Me? What did I do?"

"Get a clue, Jodi." Heather's voice dripped with sarcasm.

"Like, if you're gonna be all junior high about it . . . I happened to be with Stan when you called tonight."

Silence.

"Heather, it's not like what you're thinking."

"Really?"

"Yes, really," Jodi said. Although, if totally honest, Jodi had to admit she enjoyed the thought of being with Stan.

"Well," Heather said, "I saw how you two were acting last night. Gosh, like, I thought you were my friend."

Jodi rolled her eyes. "What in the world? So, that's why you were all rude—"

"Yeah, maybe. Sure. That's part of it."

"And? . . . What else is bothering you?"

Heather blew out a breath. "It doesn't matter."

Jodi wasn't about to press the point. If Heather didn't want to talk about something, even an act of Congress wouldn't force her to talk.

"Look, Heather, call off the attack dogs," Jodi said, wanting to smooth things over. "Just so you know, we were talking about Gus and the clinic . . . and the fact that Stan got a job there this morning and he found out all kinds of crazy stuff. *That's* why we were talking."

Neither one spoke for a full minute. Jodi picked through the ends of her hair. She knew Heather would talk when she was good and ready to say something. And if not, oh well. Jodi had plenty to do to get ready for the morning.

"Honestly? I guess your whole clinic thing bothers me," Heather said.

Jodi had guessed as much but wasn't about to interrupt.

Heather said, "Tell me, what do you really think you're going to do snooping around there? I mean, come on, abortion has been legal since before we were born. For us, it's always been that way. Do you think your crusade is gonna change that?"

"Probably not," Jodi said. "But that's not the goal."

Heather said, "Then I guess I don't see what the point is of getting all worked up over . . . that place."

"In case you missed it, this is about Faith as much as it is about what Gus said is going on with Dr. Graham."

"This is gonna sound awful," Heather said, "but as far as Faith is concerned, I think what's done is done. She made a choice . . . so this is her problem, not yours. Why can't you and Stan just let go of it?"

Jodi put the cap back on her water bottle. "Remember the story of Cain?"

"Huh?"

"The story of Cain and Abel—in Genesis? When God asked Cain about his brother, Cain said—"

Heather finished the line. "'Am I my brother's keeper?' So . . . do I get a star now?"

Jodi didn't respond.

"I'm sorry, Jodi. What's that got to do with anything?"

Jodi took a deep breath. "Faith is hurting right now. I happen to think we should do what we can to help her. I think that would bring a smile to God's face."

It was Heather's turn to be silent.

"And you're wrong about something else, Heather."

"Like what?"

"That things can't change," Jodi said. "What about Mothers Against Drunk Driving? We studied that in Mrs. Meyer's class, remember?"

"So?"

"I did a paper on them. Before MADD came on the scene, only a couple of states had anti-drunk-driving laws. But," Jodi said, thinking back to her report, "they worked to change things so that, like, all fifty states now have made it a crime to drink and drive."

"Wow, I didn't realize I was back in summer school—"

Jodi ignored the insult. "And there's Martin Luther King, who did so much for the civil rights movement. And Abe Lincoln, who helped to bring an end to slavery."

"Time out, Jodi. This isn't social studies—"

"All of them prove that bad laws can be changed when we—or somebody—stand for what's right."

"All right already," Heather said. "So, where do I go to sign up for your crusade? Got any petitions for me to circulate?"

Jodi bit her bottom lip. She was tempted to just hang up. "You know something, Heather? You're being such a dork."

"Whatever—"

"And another thing," Jodi said. "Not that you care, but it looks like Faith wasn't even pregnant when they did the procedure."

"How would you know that?"

"Stan found her file. Her pregnancy test was listed as having a 'false-positive' finding."

"Which means?"

"The results were inconclusive at best."

"So now you think that quack Gus was right—that they'd actually operate on women who aren't pregnant?"

"Looks that way," Jodi said, walking out the back door onto the deck. "I'll know for sure in the morning."

"Like how?"

"I'm going there myself—and we both know there's no way I'm pregnant."

"But," Heather said after a moment. "I don't get it. Why would they do that to you?"

"It's all about the money, Heather."

"Wait a sec," Heather said. "You may be the debate queen, but how can you say that? You don't know what their motives are."

Jodi shrugged. She switched the phone to her other ear. "Think about it. Stan told me Dr. Graham does, like, twelve aborts an hour."

"Gosh, is he sure about that?"

"He worked there today, remember?" Jodi sat down on the picnic table.

"Oh, right."

"And, when I called, they said it'll cost three hundred dollars to terminate my pregnancy," Jodi said. "Gus claims Dr. Graham gets a third of that in cash—"

"Which is one hundred dollars," Heather said.

"Times twelve. Do the math."

"Gee, you're right. That's twelve hundred dollars an hour."

"And he's not even a real doctor," Jodi said.

Neither spoke for a moment. Jodi listened to the wind chimes as they danced in the evening breeze.

"Still, even if I were to agree with you and Gus that, like, Dr. Graham is whacked, come on, Jodi. How many other clinics are like his?"

"Great question," Jodi said. "What I want to know is how many could you live with before you thought it was time to do something?"

Gus finished eating at the burger joint next to his hotel. He paid and then shuffled back to his room. He had specifically requested room 101 in the two-story building. It had been a Days Inn years ago. Now everything about the place was tired and worn.

The new owners had renamed it Night-Night Inn and spent as little as possible to remodel. They tossed a coat of fresh paint on the walls, reglazed the tubs, and cleaned the carpets. The in-room phones still had the original Days Inn placard around their rotary dials.

Gus walked into the lobby. He noticed the attendant, a man of about three hundred pounds, was watching TV. Gus stopped at the front desk and waited. After a long minute, he rang the bell and then rested his palms on the counter.

The attendant turned around. "Gus, my man, whaz-up?"

"My man . . . ," Gus repeated. "Did you mail my letter . . . my man?"

"That greasy thing? I'd be surprised if the postman would touch it, what with all them anthrax scares." He leaned over and checked the slot for outgoing mail. "Well, look at that . . . yes-sir-ee, Bob. It's gone."

Gus's head jerked to the left, then the right. "Bob? I'm Gus."

He laughed. He turned back to his show. "Chill, my man. It's just a saying."

Gus considered this. He pulled on his beard as he walked toward his room. "A saying . . . just a saying . . . we're all just saying . . . my man."

Gus returned to his room. He opened the door and noticed the bed had been made. Puzzled, he looked at the door to see if the Do Not Disturb sign was still hanging from the handle. It was. With a grunt, he closed the door.

Once inside, he turned off the noisy air conditioner, pulled back the tattered drapes, opened the window, and lingered by the screen for a moment. A blanket of soft, black clouds muzzled the moon, choking off most of its dim reflection. The sound of a passing truck on Easton Road interrupted the chorus of crickets.

He wandered over to the floor lamp and clicked it off. He moved toward the bed and, with a click, turned off the wall-mounted lamp to the left of the headboard. A sodium-vapor streetlight at the edge of the parking lot cast a wisp of light into his otherwise dark space.

He sat down on the edge of the queen-size bed, removed his shoes, and, without undressing further, lay on top of the covers. His head fell against the pillow. In the near darkness he folded his hands across his chest and stared at the barely visible cottage cheese–like formations on the ceiling.

It was nice of them to have provided a hotel, such as it was. Had it really been almost two months since he first checked in? The place was starting to feel like home.

Home.

It had been years since he'd had a home.

Back in Maryland.

Back where it had all started.

And ended.

Back before they took it all away. He tried to picture his mansion in Annapolis, Maryland, home for the better part of twenty years, but nothing came. He was losing his mind, that much was sure. He even had difficulty recalling his ex-wife's face. In an odd sort of way, he couldn't remember the things he loved, just the things he hated.

He had lost his home.

He had lost his wife.

He had lost his career.

And now he was losing his marbles.

If only he could lose the guilt.

Gus closed his eyes, as if doing so would shut out the past. Within moments, he struggled to control his breathing as the memories, like a parade, marched into his mind.

He was in his late twenties, an idealist, and fresh out of medical school when he met and married his wife, Vikki, a hippie leftover who became a women's rights activist. He remembered her excitement when the U.S. Supreme Court handed down its verdict in the *Roe* v. *Wade* case, which happened to coincide with the year he received his medical certification.

At the urging of Vikki, and not wanting to disappoint his new bride, he had opened the first women's health clinic in Annapolis to provide women a safe, professional environment to terminate their unwanted pregnancies. With the blessing of the law, he was convinced he was acting in the best interest of women.

Business had been good.

Almost too good.

Within three years, it was so good, he couldn't keep up with the demand.

Over a heaping plate of spicy wings and beer, he had explained his dilemma to a former college roommate, Victor Graham. Vic, who had graduated with a marketing degree, worked across town in his parents' funeral home where, as Vic used to joke, people were dying to get in.

Gus couldn't recall whether it had been his or Vic's idea to become partners. It didn't matter. Gus never should have compromised his training, his ideals, and his medical practice by opening the door to Vic. Even now, Gus dragged with him the weight of that fateful decision like a ball and chain around his legs.

By the end of the meal, Vic had convinced Gus to show him the ropes. After all, Vic had argued, how difficult would it be to do the same thing ten times an hour? This wasn't like brain surgery. When Gus balked, citing the need for a medical license, Vic had said, "As if anybody needs to know—besides, we have yours hanging on the wall. That's good enough."

Vic had proved to be a fast study, a hard worker, and a skilled liar. It was Vic who cooked up a scheme to advertise Gus's clinic under thirty different names in order to attract different segments of the market—with all the phone numbers linked to one central facility.

Vic had been quick to give a five-dollar incentive to the clinic's phone operators for each client they successfully talked into a procedure. He had posted signs on each phone that read, "The call you miss, our competition gets." And it was Vic who had hatched the idea of the low-dose birth-control pills to "stimulate repeat business."

The best part, according to Vic, was that they had become millionaires by age thirty. To top it off, Vic had devised a system where they were paid in cash at the end of each day for the number of pregnancies terminated.

Once again, Vic had beat the system.

Cash was king.

And, with no W-2 forms, no 1099 forms, and no set of official figures turned in to the IRS, they could report whatever income they wanted and avoid paying added income taxes.

Vic was spinning out of control, and Gus knew it but didn't put the brakes on him. Half the time, Gus found himself warning Vic to slow down, to be more precise when determining the gestational age of the fetus—or, during the pelvic examination, to make sure the woman was even pregnant.

Vic wouldn't hear of it.

He was too busy overcharging the government for Title X funds, the taxpayer funds that were supposed to be used for the care of the poor. Vic cooked the books and soaked the government by billing it two to four times what a cash-paying customer was actually charged for the services. Who would ever know? The government was nothing more than a big, bloated, incompetent collection of bureaucrats.

When the State of Maryland first investigated the clinic based upon a complaint filed with the Health and Human Services Department, Gus knew something drastic needed to be done.

He immediately confronted Vic about the shady dealings.

About the premature shredding of files.

About falsifying vital signs, if providing them at all.

About Vic's pet dog who, on more than one occasion, licked the floor clean at the end of a day.

Vic, who had become so cocky and so verbally abusive even members of the staff were complaining, dismissed the whole inquiry as a joke. Vic hired the most expensive lawyer in town, and the charges were dismissed. He returned to business as usual and dreamed of franchising the clinic.

Gus couldn't pinpoint the exact moment he had snapped. But somewhere along the way, Vic's arguments about women's rights, freedom of choice, and compassionate care got lost in the business of making money.

Big money. Blood money.

Back then and late at night, in the rare moments when he wasn't reaching for a bottle of alcohol to escape, Gus conceded that the fight over *Roe* v. *Wade* was really about preserving a way of life for an industry—his industry—one that profited from the pain of those it served.

Although he didn't consider himself to be pro-life, he couldn't live with the dishonesty of his own idealism any longer. He had lost all respect for his profession and didn't want to be associated with it any longer.

That realization, together with an out-of-control partner, was the final straw. Gus ended his partnership with Vic and left the business in order to take some time to rethink his priorities.

Vic made sure that wasn't an option.

Vic phoned in an anonymous tip to the IRS about Gus's unpaid back taxes. Overnight, the IRS seized Gus's home, boat, and cars, and froze his stocks and bank accounts. Stunned and wounded by the sudden loss of everything she had, Vikki left Gus.

Homeless, Gus took to the streets where, for the better part of a decade, he somehow survived as he followed the movements of Vic, who ran from the law in Maryland, to Delaware, and then to Pennsylvania.

But when Gus went to collect a Social Security check in Philadelphia, the IRS, like a six-hundred-pound gorilla, ambushed him. They threatened him with a heavy jail sentence unless he cooperated by turning on his old partner.

Gus rolled to his side and, with his back to the window, curled up into the fetal position.

What he wouldn't give for a little peace of mind.

Or just one peaceful night's sleep.

And yet somehow he believed the nightmare would be over any day now. It had to be. He was sure of it. Once the truth about Victor Graham was revealed and the IRS goons were finally off his back, he'd be free.

Gus closed his eyes. It felt good to be off his feet. His shoes had several holes in the bottom, and a blister was forming on his right big toe. With a tug, he pulled a pillow from underneath the covers and snuggled it against his chest. The scent of a freshly washed pillowcase greeted his nose. He felt the tension start to drain from his limbs, and his breathing slowed. Even the burning sensation from behind his tired eyes seemed to cool.

Eyes still closed, he rolled over onto his other side, facing the window. As he shifted his weight on the bed, the pillow fell over the edge and onto the floor.

"Here, let me help you with that," a voice said from somewhere in the darkness.

About all Gus caught was a glimpse of the silhouette of his assailant before the pillow was shoved, with the force of a trash compactor, over his face. Strong arms held the pillow in place, his mouth and nose buried. His mind raced for an explanation.

This had to be one of the wrong people.

Gus kicked and twisted his tired legs, trying to break free. His heart beat wildly at the unexpected attack. Like a crazed animal, Gus clawed at the pillow. His lungs burned, starved for even an ounce of precious air.

Through the layers of polyester filling that encased his world, he heard a muffled voice say, "I'm going to release you in a moment. I don't want to hear even a peep—or I *will* kill you."

Gus struggled for another couple of seconds. On the verge of passing out, he fell deathly still. He waited for what felt like an eternity before the pillow was raised. He gulped air like a thirsty man gulps water in the desert. As his lungs worked overtime to replenish the stolen breaths, he tried to focus on the towering figure over him.

The invader was dressed in black and wore a ski mask over his face. He stood motionless, ready to pounce again, of that Gus was sure. Out of the corner of his eye, a glint of light from the reluctant moon reflected off an object in the man's hand.

At first the item hadn't registered.

He squinted. No mistake now.

A scalpel.

Not much of a weapon for a layman. But, as Gus knew all too well, in the hands of a trained person, the thin, sharp blade might as well be a butcher's knife.

"Roll over, facedown," the man commanded.

With a yank, the mugger wrapped a blindfold around Gus's head. He pulled the bandaging tighter before tying a knot at the back of his head. Gus felt his temples throbbing against the bindings.

The assailant jerked Gus's arms backward. "Don't move," he said, now taping together his wrists with duct tape. Gus groaned as the hair on the back of his hands was snagged by the tape adhesive. Gus, still facedown on the bed, heard another strip of tape being pulled from the roll.

"Answer me this," the man said in a low, cold tone. "Where's the videotape?"

Gus, his nose smashed against the bed, mumbled an answer through his beard, its thicket of hairs soaked with a mixture of sweat and saliva.

The man smacked the side of Gus's head. The spot where his hand made contact stung as if attacked by hornets. "Speak up when I ask you a question."

Gus wanted to swallow, but no moisture remained in his throat. "Mail. I . . . mailed."

"You stupid, worthless bum."

Another smack, this time to the base of the neck. A gush of air escaped Gus's open mouth.

"Where did you mail it?"

"Newspaper . . . up the street . . . the right people."

Gus knew there was no point hiding the truth. Not from this man. He knew the intruder had to be Victor Graham. In fact, Gus had figured it would be only a matter of time before Vic came here to get the video after what Gus had said in his letter. Oddly, he had almost hoped Vic *would* come, make a scene, and even kidnap him.

What better way to prove the man's guilt.

He got his wish.

Dr. Graham used the tape to muzzle Gus's mouth. He seized Gus by the arm and, with a pull, said, "Stand up, scumbag. We're going for a drive."

Gus, blindfolded, gagged, and with his hands tied together at the wrists, shuffled forward, shoeless. He heard the door to the room open. He sensed Vic standing still by the door, probably to make sure nobody was around.

With a sudden pull on his arm, Gus lurched forward, stumbling blindly into the hall. More prodding. They turned left and then outside through a side entrance. They went a few steps more and then halted as Vic, still holding his arm, abruptly stopped.

A car door opened.

"Get in."

Gus stumbled into the seat. Pain shot though his shoulder blades as his arms, still bound behind him, were wedged against the seat. The door closed. Gus felt Victor's face hovering like a gnat next to his right ear. Vic spoke just above a whisper.

"Tell me, Gus, have you ever been deep-sea diving?"

Nothing but a patchwork of off-white clouds, accented with the occasional thread of gray, blanketed the morning sky. While it looked like a storm was brewing, no rain was mentioned in the forecast. In a way, Jodi was thankful for the overcast sky. It felt appropriate. Like Stan, she felt she, too, was going over to the dark side.

At the crack of dawn, Jodi had hit the floor running. For starters, she figured she needed to dress the part. She wanted to look like a pregnant, worried, teen girl. She was both a teen and a girl, so that much was easily covered. And she felt sure she had the worried part down pat.

After all, she had spent much of the night stressing out about her decision to go. What if they saw through her act? Would they throw her out? Would they call the police? What if they hauled her off and tossed her in some prison cell at the South Pole for the rest of her life?

Okay, so that was an overreaction. Still, she didn't think it would be difficult to look worried.

As for being pregnant, she had settled on loose jeans, a simple, oversize black top, plain earrings, sneakers—didn't pregnant women always seem to wear sneakers?—and dark sunglasses, which, she figured, suggested anonymity. She wore a hint of makeup and pulled her hair back, bunching it up at the back of her head, holding it in place with a hook and pin.

She had opted for a saddlebag-style purse, which had plenty of room for Stan's urine sample and her dad's voice-activated, microcassette player with fresh batteries.

Jodi turned her car onto the street where the clinic was located. According to the map, the Total Choice Medi-Center was situated on the border between Philadelphia and an affluent suburb. She checked the street numbers. Stan had said it was a two-story building adjacent to a small, professional center with plenty of parking.

Her heart was pounding, her hands moist on the steering wheel. She was really doing this. She was about to enter another world. Like Dorothy in *The Wizard of Oz*, she felt like saying, "Toto, we're not in Kansas anymore."

As the building came into view, two things struck her. The building wasn't the sleaze joint she had envisioned. It was a well-maintained facility with manicured landscaping. She also saw a small parade of people with placards and handmade signs strolling up and down the sidewalk in front of it. A picket line? Great.

She pulled into the parking lot, parked and locked the car, slipped on her sunglasses, draped her purse over her shoulder, and headed for the sidewalk. Although nobody was blocking the sidewalk, she noticed the only way to the front door was to walk past the two dozen or so protesters.

Her heart leaped. These pro-life advocates were going to think she was there to get an abortion. Now what? How could she explain what she was really doing without blowing her cover? If she remained silent, for all she knew someone from her church might be milling about in the crowd.

She could imagine the rumors in youth group on Sunday.

Suddenly, her coming to this place wasn't such a simple matter of doing background research for her story. At the same time, it was too late to turn back. She planted a smile on her face and then started down the sidewalk, which ran parallel to the street.

The goose bumps popping up all over her body didn't help. She blew out a breath to control her anxiety.

As she approached, a nun on her right was praying the rosary. Just beyond her, a couple wore matching T-shirts with the words "Life:

What a beautiful choice." A mother with two kids in a stroller held up a poster that read, "Children are a gift from the Lord."

A sign mounted on a stick, bobbing up and down, caught her attention: "Thank God your mother was pro-life." Someone else held a sign saying, "God loves you . . . and your unborn baby, too."

Moving past the first few people was easy enough. Their smiles were warm and inviting. The faces of the little ones were the most irresistible. A toddler with round, red cheeks waved. Jodi, unsure how to respond, smiled, cupped her hand, and gave a half-wave back. She walked on. As she did, she overheard several people whispering prayers.

"May she change her mind . . ."

"Give her courage to love her baby even now . . ."

"Lead us not into temptation, but deliver us from evil."

How she wished she could assure these dear ones that she wasn't here for the reason most women came to this building. She admired their efforts and wanted to say, "I'm on your side . . . I'm not even pregnant . . ."

Instead, she ducked her head. Not in shame, but to keep from engaging the protesters. She didn't want to compromise the whole point of her being there. Several steps more and she'd be through what felt like a minefield filled with hidden explosives.

She walked on, and the posters bounced with urgency.

It wasn't hot, but Jodi felt herself breaking out in a cold sweat. She seemed to move in slow motion, as if in a dreamlike state. Each step felt more difficult than the one before it, as if the sidewalk were suddenly rising uphill beneath her.

Another ten steps or so and she'd be able to turn left toward the building. She heard, and then saw, a man in his mid-thirties break away from the others. His face was puckered as if he had sucked on a lemon. He wagged a finger at Jodi. He chanted, "Baby killer . . . baby killer . . . baby killer."

Jodi stopped in her tracks; her heart ran wild.

Unlike the others, who protested in relative silence, this man actually scared her. His eyes narrowed; his face reddened. One of the others tried to pull him back in line. He yanked his arm free and stepped closer to Jodi.

Jodi gripped her purse in front of her as if it would keep the angry man at a safe distance. Shaken, Jodi started to walk again. *Just get me there.* She found herself longing to reach the safety of the clinic's front door.

*How ironic,* she thought. Before she had arrived, she'd viewed the clinic as some sort of dragon to be slain. Now, with this monster in her face, the clinic seemed almost like a place of refuge. *Gosh, do I ever sound like that?*

The man continued his chant: "Baby hater . . . baby killer . . . baby murderer . . ."

Jodi couldn't contain herself anymore. She marched five steps over to the man and, bracing herself, said, "Listen, buddy, whatever happened to 'They'll know we are Christians by our love'? Or, did you forget that part?" She thought she heard the nun behind her say, "Amen."

The man's beet-red face looked as if it would explode. Jodi felt a hand squeeze her arm. The hand tugged gently at her as a voice said, "Come with me, sweetheart. I'm with the women's center. I'm sorry about that."

Jodi threw one last laser blast at the man with her eyes over the top of her sunglasses before turning to follow the clinic worker.

At the front door, Jodi noticed a security camera. The worker rang the bell. An instant later and with a buzz, the security lock yielded. Jodi was ushered through the front door. It closed behind her with a soft thud.

"I'm sorry about that. Don't worry; we've already called the cops. Now, how can we be of service?"

Jodi removed her glasses. She was inside. She was also ready to leave. An inner voice was screaming, "Run!" As she struggled to silence her fears, she realized she hadn't prayed before coming. She whispered, "Jesus, be with me . . . now!"

"Miss?"

Jodi wrung her hands as she said, "Oh, sorry. I'm here to see . . . Delores. We talked yesterday."

"If you'll have a seat, I'll get Delores."

Jodi moved to a row of chairs but remained standing. She reminded herself she was here as a reporter and needed to gather as many details as possible. The sparsely decorated space was clean, comfortable, and devoid of any medical licenses hanging on the wall. She made a mental note.

A black woman in a floral dress, Jodi guessed in her late thirties, came to the counter. "I'm Delores . . . you must be Jodi."

Jodi clung to her purse and offered a weak smile. "That's me." She reached inside her purse and, with a flick of a switch, carefully clicked on her recorder.

"Very good. I'm so glad you came," Delores said. "If you'll come with me and have a seat over here." With the wave of a hand, she motioned Jodi around the corner of the reception counter to what looked like a consultation area. The walls were painted a relaxing beige, the trim and doors a warm burgundy with navy blue accents. Very classy.

Jodi did as instructed. As she sat, she placed her purse on the desk and then folded her hands in her lap. She heard a door open behind her. She looked over her shoulder, hoping to see Stan with his big, beaming smile walk through the door. The thought was comforting. Instead, a nervous-looking girl was escorted to an adjacent consultation booth.

Jodi had never felt so alone.

On the second floor of the Total Choice Medi-Center, Dr. Graham paced behind his desk like a caged tiger. With a phone glued to his ear, he had stopped counting after ten rings. Through a clenched jaw, he muttered, "Where is she? Why isn't she answering?"

Jenna hadn't shown on the boat for dinner last night. He was infuriated. He could understand how a last-minute conflict might prevent her from coming, but there was no excuse—none whatsoever—for not calling. She had all his numbers, including the number for the phone on the boat.

Granted, the evening hadn't been a complete waste. He was confident he had Joey Stephano sufficiently tucked away in his back pocket. And he had Gus tucked away in one of the boat's lower storage compartments. Dr. Graham knew he had to somehow put his hands on Gus's video. Once the tape was safely in hand, he'd be free to send Gus swimming in the ocean.

Naturally, he would hire a couple of hoodlums to do the dirty work. But not yet. Dr. Graham had no choice but to keep Gus alive just in case the old fool lied about where he had mailed the video. Besides, at the moment, he was preoccupied with the fact that Jenna hadn't come to work and hadn't called in sick.

"Answer your phone, Jenna."

After a dozen rings, he banged down the phone, poured a drink, and then dialed another number, this time to his lawyer in Maryland. He answered on the first ring.

"Hello?"

Dr. Graham barked, "I've got a situation."

"Yes?"

"My ex-partner did a stupid thing. A very stupid thing."

"What now?"

"A video. He has—or had—a videotape made without me knowing about it . . . until now."

"Of what? A romp with an employee?"

"No. Worse. Remember the Casey situation?"

The lawyer whistled. "He has *that* on film?"

"So he says." Dr. Graham swore. "He gave me a letter and claimed he filmed everything."

Just before Gus had resigned from his partnership with Vic, Dr. Graham had accidentally delivered a live, late-term baby. His first mistake was to have improperly assessed the age of the unborn baby. The couple said it was twenty-six weeks, but upon delivery, the fetus turned out to be closer to thirty-four weeks.

It wasn't supposed to live, but it did.

The baby's cry had been unmistakable. Dr. Graham had been paid handsomely by the wealthy couple to terminate, and failure wasn't an option. He dismissed his two assistants and, with nobody watching—or so he thought—he finished what he had been paid to do.

But it didn't end there. Having heard the cry of the baby silenced, the patient filed a lawsuit citing infanticide and asked for ten million dollars in emotional damages. The case had been dismissed on grounds of insufficient evidence.

It was a case of his word against hers.

The prospect of this videotape falling into the wrong hands sent a chill down his spine.

After a minute, his lawyer asked, "Blackmail?"

"More like revenge. He's mad at me for sicking the IRS dogs onto his trail. So now he's played his trump card."

"I see. Where is he?"

Dr. Graham took a sip from his glass tumbler. "Let's just say he's . . . *contained*."

A silence passed between them.

"What about the tape?"

Dr. Graham swore again. "He mailed it to the local newspaper." He took another drink. "What are my options? Can you throw an injunction against them . . . I don't know, something that keeps them from opening the stolen property?"

"Look, Vic, I'll try anything, you know that, but . . ."

"But what?"

"I don't think we have time . . . and if we did, good luck trying to enforce it."

Dr. Graham's intercom buzzed. "Hold on," he said to the lawyer. He punched a button. "Yes?"

"We're ready for you—"

He snapped. "Where's Jenna? Has she called?"

"No, sir."

Dr. Graham squeezed the base of his neck as he considered the options. "Send that new kid in here—what's his name?"

"Stan Taylor."

"Yes. Do it. And I'll come down when I'm good and ready." He punched the blinking line on hold. "I'm back."

"Look, Vic, just an idea, but do you know anybody over at the newspaper you could approach?"

Dr. Graham massaged his temples. "Just had dinner with the owner last night."

"Perfect. Call him—"

"And tell him what? Tell him he's likely to be receiving evidence of a murder but that he should ignore it?" He hit the top of his desk with a fist. "You're dumber than I thought."

"Vic, shut up and listen—"

Dr. Graham ground his teeth. "No, *you* listen to *me*, you overpaid, good-for-nothing idiot. You find a way—a legally binding remedy—to impound that tape. And do it this instant."

He slammed down the phone, his lungs laboring beneath his chest. His right hand shook as he reached for his glass. Running his left hand through his hair, he sipped his drink and then, using the speakerphone, dialed Jenna's number.

Two rings. Three rings. Five rings. No answer.

He heard a knock at the door.

"What is it?" Dr. Graham asked, ending the call.

"It's Stan. You wanted to see me?"

Dr. Graham searched his face. To be sure, the kid was wet behind the ears. But he appeared to be smarter than most. Surely he could follow simple instructions.

"You got a car, kid?"

"Sure do."

"Then do this," Dr. Graham said. He scribbled a note on a piece of paper. "That's Jenna's apartment address. You met her yesterday," he said without looking up.

"Uh-huh."

"Look, I want you to drive over there. She's at the Village Manor Apartments," Dr. Graham said, handing Stan the paper. "You know where that is, right?"

Stan looked at the directions. "Sure thing."

"Tell her . . . tell her she's needed at work."

"Now?" Stan said, pointing toward the door.

"Yes, now."

"Sir, should I call first? Maybe—"

Dr. Graham snarled. "Don't be stupid. Her phone isn't working. That's why you're going over there. Now, if you'll excuse me, we're short-handed and I've got a building full of patients."

Jodi's nervous system was on maximum spin. Everything had gone pretty much as she'd expected. The pregnancy test was "inconclusive," so Delores requested a urine sample. Jodi had carefully poured Stan's sample into the cup and then tried to avoid looking as guilty as she felt when she handed the specimen to Delores.

The in-house lab results came back in a brisk fifteen minutes indicating that, yes, Jodi was most likely eight to ten weeks pregnant. Delores had explained that, in these iffy situations, a final confirmation would be made by the doctor during a pelvic exam.

All included in the price.

Jodi lay on the examination table in room 1, as immobile as her pounding heart would permit. She had changed into a tentlike, faded green hospital gown. Her purse, shoes, pants, and personal effects were bundled together and rested on the stainless steel counter at her side.

The anticipation of meeting Dr. Graham, and of just lying on the table where so many lost their chance at life, was almost unbearable. Worse, the idea of this man giving her a pelvic exam was beyond humiliating. She wished she could close her eyes, tap her heels together three times, and wake up in the safety of her bedroom.

She knew to get to the truth, she needed to swallow her pride and, at least for several seconds, surrender her modesty while the doctor probed. She folded her hands across her stomach and started to pray, "Lord, I can't do this . . ." She had barely begun to pray when Dr. Graham zoomed into the room, two medical assistants following in his wake.

All three wore white surgical masks and skullcaps.

An odd sensation resonated in the back of her mind. She couldn't pinpoint the source of her impression. But it struck Jodi that they wore their masks for the same reason the Lone Ranger wore his—to conceal his true identity.

Bingo.

Stan mentioned he was never to call Dr. Graham by name.

She studied their appearance. No name tags. Not that she expected Dr. Graham to wear a peel'n'stick label that read, "Hi. My name is Dr. Death." Still, as far as she could remember, even Delores never called Dr. Graham by name. She thought, *Let's see if he at least introduces himself.*

Dr. Graham snapped his fingers with impatience. The assistant produced Jodi's paperwork attached to a clipboard. He snatched it, scanned it, and handed it back.

"Let's see what we've got, sweetie."

*Sweetie?*

Dr. Graham approached the table, pulling on a pair of surgical gloves. She thought she caught a whiff of alcohol hiding behind a heavy dose of mouthwash. He placed a hand on her stomach and pressed down. Jodi stiffened, as if confronted by a rattlesnake.

"Relax, honey." He glanced under the sheet. She felt the touch of his frosty hands and fought the urge to vomit. She fully expected him to say, "There's nothing in here."

Instead, Dr. Graham straightened and approached her side. "You're an easy nine weeks along. So, you've been a bad little girl? No problem. We'll get you cleaned out in no time, baby doll."

*Bad little girl? Baby doll?*

She was repulsed by his arrogant, godlike attitude. It was as if all the awful things she had ever heard from Gus about this man collided together in a single moment. Maybe it was a lack of sleep. Maybe a case of nerves. Probably both. In any event, she felt mad enough to kick Dr. Graham with both feet.

He turned to his assistant and said, "Catheter."

The worker readied the machine.

Jodi's heart was about to burst. This guy wasn't kidding around. He was really going ahead with the procedure. Her head felt light and she thought she would pass out. Under no circumstances could she afford to faint. He'd be done before she'd awaken. Dizzy, as if she had stepped off a roller coaster, she propped herself up on an elbow.

"You sure, Doctor? I . . . I don't have any morning sickness and, like, I'm not tired or anything like that—"

"Lay down, sweet cakes," Dr. Graham said. "You're just one fertile little turtle." He took the suction catheter, its three-quarter-inch, sharp, snakelike head ready to bite, from an assistant. The machine moaned and howled like a hungry dog waiting for its next meal.

Jodi's chest heaved as she tried to catch her breath. "Listen, I . . . I just can't go through with this—"

"Relax, missy," Dr. Graham said, his eyebrows narrowing. "You'll hardly feel a thing." He was positioning the vacuum tube when Jodi shot upright.

"Stop it! Stop it! I'm not pregnant!" She even shocked herself with the outburst. The words seemed to bounce around the walls for five full seconds.

Dr. Graham peered over his face mask, motionless. She couldn't tell what he was thinking, but somehow she knew it wasn't very flattering.

"I'm a reporter for the *Montgomery Times,* and you, Dr. Graham, just blew it big time."

Dr. Graham lowered the suction catheter, turned off the machine, and then raised his right forefinger. "Does anybody in here know what this kid is saying?"

No one spoke.

He turned to the first assistant. "What just happened?"

"Sir, nothing. You just gave her a pelvic exam and informed her that she wasn't pregnant."

Jodi said, "What in the world?"

"And you?" Dr. Graham said to the second assistant. "What did you see?"

The nervous-looking woman rocked in place. "Like she said, you did the pelvic and found nothing. That's it."

"Well, then," he said, consulting the chart, "Jodi Adams. Looks like I have two witnesses who disagree with your fabrication of events."

Jodi was about to scream. She pulled herself up to a sitting position and started to say something, but Dr. Graham cut her off.

"Now, missy, I'd suggest you gather your things, dress quietly, and go back to your trailer park." When Jodi didn't immediately move, he added, "Get out of my place of business before I call the cops. And, if I hear so much as another word out of your lying mouth, I will sue you."

Jodi found the air in the room too thick to breathe. She struggled to fill her lungs. Her heart hammered so hard her chest ached. Moving in slow motion, she slid off the examination table, still draped in her gown. She reached for her things, watching Dr. Graham out of the corner of her eye as she gathered her valuables.

"Oh, but that's where you're wrong, *Mister* Graham," Jodi said, pushing her way past the two assistants. "Way wrong. Gus was right—you're nothing more than a fraud, and I can prove it."

"Get out!" Dr. Graham said, his eyes blazing.

Jodi stood in the doorway. She tapped her purse. "I have it all recorded on tape. Every last word."

Dr. Graham's face turned white and then red.

Jodi had never seen such rage pour out of a man's eyes before. Like a refugee fleeing the long arm of a militant dictator, she darted down the hall. Juggling her clothes, purse, and shoes in her arms, she saw a door at the very end of the fifty-foot hall marked "Emergency Exit Only." She raced to it as if her life depended on it.

Her ankles felt like an invisible set of hands had reached up from the floor and grabbed them, holding her back, keeping her from leaving the belly of the beast. Behind her, she heard Dr. Graham barking commands to his minions.

In her haste, she dropped her purse.

Jodi backtracked five steps, scrambled to pick it up, dropped a shoe, grabbed it, and, looking up, saw the two assistants starting toward her. She turned and galloped toward the door. She shoved an elbow against the crash bar, almost losing her balance in the process. An earsplitting alarm sounded as the door opened to freedom.

Barefoot and scared, Jodi bolted to her car. The loose driveway gravel, like coarse sandpaper, grated the bottoms of her feet. She jumped to avoid a patch of shattered glass but managed to stub a toe when she landed. A moment later, she reached her car.

She fumbled inside the purse for her keys, found them, beeped and unlocked the door, tossed her things across the front seat, and jumped in, whacking her shin against the threshold. She slammed and locked the door, jammed the key in the ignition, and prayed the car would start.

With a roar, the engine sprang to life. Thankful for small miracles, she slammed it into gear and pulled away.

In the distance, Jodi heard a police siren. She wasn't sure whether or not they were coming for her.

She wasn't about to stick around and find out.

ꝋ

Dr. Graham raced to his office and closed the door. He didn't stop to pour a drink. Time was of the essence. Using the preset speed dial on his cell phone, he placed the call.

A young man answered. "Yo."

Dr. Graham said, "Change of plans."

"I'm listening."

"Got another fish that needs to go swimming tonight."

"Details?"

"The name's Jodi Adams. Blonde. About five-five. Maybe seventeen."

"Sounds nice."

"Shut up and listen. Drives a white Mazda. Works at the *Montgomery Times*."

"When?"

Dr. Graham reached for a bottle of bourbon and a glass. "Pick her up this afternoon."

"No problem."

"One more thing."

"Name it."

"She has an audiotape you must—I repeat, *must*—find and bring to me."

"Done."

Stan hiked three flights of stairs, two steps at a time. This whole thing of going to Jenna's apartment was weird. Maybe Jenna was tired of Dr. Graham's tantrums. Maybe she needed a break from his rudeness and the constant barking of commands. The fact that he had major control issues was clear to Stan after just one day.

Imagine working for the tyrant for years!

And that was the strange part. Why did she put up with him for so long? She seemed nice enough, even approachable. Unlike Dr. Graham, she was soft-spoken and her eyes brimmed with a surprising warmth. Her working at the clinic made no sense as far as Stan could tell.

Although yesterday he didn't mind being Dr. Graham's gofer, he resented the fact that he had been thrown into the middle of things with Jenna today. If she didn't want to come to work, that was her choice, right? Then again, as unlikely as it seemed, maybe Dr. Graham was just concerned about her welfare.

Stan reached the third floor. Four apartment doors faced each other in a quad-shaped courtyard. He checked the apartment number inked on his palm and then scanned the doors. He found the winning number. He took a second to catch his breath. Even in the heart of football season, dashing up that many stairs would be a workout.

Pausing by her front door, he noticed a black-and-red welcome mat. To the left, a three-foot-tall frilly, plantlike thing with small flowers was growing in a ceramic pot. *Definitely something a girl would get,* he thought.

Miniblinds hung in a window to the right of the door. Although drawn tight, a space at the bottom permitted him a partial view of the stainless steel kitchen sink. It was empty. Maybe she wasn't home. There was one way to find out. Stan looked for the doorbell. Finding none, he tapped out a friendly rhythm with a knuckle.

No answer. He put an eyeball to the security peephole as if somehow he could look in. No such luck. He knocked again and then put his hands in his front pockets. What if she didn't answer? He could leave a note but didn't have pen and paper. He knocked a third time.

Stan turned to go. Behind him and through the closed door he heard a voice.

"Who is it?"

Stan faced the door. "It's me, Stan . . . Stan Taylor, from work." It felt odd to admit the clinic was where he worked.

Jenna cracked the door open three inches. The brass security chain prevented the door from opening farther. She spoke in hushed tones as if medicated. "Oh, hi, Stan. What a surprise."

Jenna looked a mess. She wore no makeup. Her hair looked tangled and unkempt. She wore a wrinkled sweatshirt and shorts. But her eyelids, puffy and red, told the real story. She had been crying.

"Gosh, Jenna, you okay?"

He thought she nodded.

"I'm sorry to hassle you at home . . ."

She pushed a stray hair from her face. "It's okay, really. I take it the big, bad boss sent you?" She smirked.

"How'd you guess?" Stan smiled back then shifted his feet. "Look, Jenna, Dr. Graham was, uh, concerned."

"Guess there's a first time for everything," she said dryly.

"Yeah, well, he really needs you at work today. He tried calling, but your phone—"

"The answering machine isn't working, and I'm not answering it."

"Oh. What should I tell him?"

"Tell him . . . ," she started to say. Her features seemed to drift into the distance. "Tell him I'm not coming back."

"Today?"

"Ever."

Stan put his hands back in his pockets.

"Listen, Stan, this has been a long time coming. And yesterday . . . when you asked about shredding the files—"

"The ones that hadn't expired?"

"Right. I guess . . . that was the last straw for me. I'm done working for that man."

Stan cleared his throat. "Okay. So, I'll tell him you quit. But he won't be happy."

"Is he ever?"

Jodi arrived at the newspaper fifteen minutes late. She would have been on time had it not been for the thirty minutes she had spent in the shower after racing home from the clinic. She had hoped the scorching stream of water would scrub away the memory of her encounter with Dr. Graham. No such luck.

During her shower, she remembered something else from Gus's letter. He had claimed that on more than one occasion, Dr. Graham had suffocated an infant who survived a procedure. When Jodi first read his accusation, she thought it was the most ludicrous thing she had ever heard. After this morning, she could believe Gus.

While she didn't have proof he was guilty of infanticide, she had no doubt Dr. Graham was capable of doing anything. After all, he was willing to perform an abortion procedure on a girl who wasn't even pregnant.

What else would he do for money?

If only she could convince Joey to let her do the story. She had the facts. She had the proof. She had two credible witnesses. What more could he want?

Jodi breezed through the front doors as if propelled by a gust of wind. Her adrenaline was maxed out from the morning, and she was itching to tell Joey about her undercover work.

"Where's the fire, Jodi?" Marge said, her glasses hanging on the tip of her nose. She was juggling a stack of files and mail.

Jodi was so preoccupied with the goal of reaching her desk, she almost bowled Marge over. Jodi slowed, turned around, but kept walking backward to her cubicle. "Oops. Sorry, Marge. Things are just a little crazy—"

"I heard that," Marge said. "Hate to slow you down, but you've got some fan mail."

Jodi stopped in her tracks.

"Me?"

"You are Jodi Adams, right?" Marge shuffled through the stack of mail and picked out a one-inch-thick, padded yellow envelope.

"Wow. Who's it from?" Jodi walked toward Marge.

"Loverboy—"

"Huh?" Jodi said, her face intense.

"Relax. It's from your pal Gus."

Jodi's heart jumped as if shocked by a blast of electricity. Marge handed her the package with a smirk.

"Heavy, too. Maybe it's chocolate."

"Thanks, Marge. I'll save you some." With that, Jodi darted to her desk.

Marge called after her, "Joey's been looking for you . . . he wanted to see you the second you got in."

Jodi called over her shoulder, "I'm on my way."

At her desk, Jodi dumped Gus's package and her purse in the bottom desk drawer. She snatched her cassette recorder and promptly plopped down in her chair. Everything was happening way too fast. She'd been running since the crack of dawn and needed two seconds to pull herself together.

It was then she noticed that two items had been placed in her in-box. An envelope and a copy of their morning paper. Who had time to read the paper? She reached for the letter. Her first name was typed on the outside. Beneath her name appeared the words: PERSONAL AND CONFIDENTIAL.

Upon opening the letter, the distinct smell of cigarette smoke floated out. The brief, four-line message had been typed in all caps:

FOLLOW THE MONEY
SEE BACK PAGE OF PAPER
THINK PER INQUIRY
CONNECT THE DOTS

The note was unsigned, and yet the smell of smoke was all the signature Jodi needed. It had to be from Roxanne. Roxanne handled the books. So, "follow the money" probably had to do with their finances.

Jodi then reached for the newspaper, unfolded it, and shuffled to the back page. Her face flushed. There, in living color, was a full-page ad for the Total Choice Medi-Center. No wonder Joey didn't want to do a story on health violations at women's clinics. A story like that could offend an advertiser—especially this one.

It made perfect sense. Still, she thought it stunk.

But what did Roxanne mean about "per inquiry"? She remembered hearing the phrase before—recently, in fact. Come to think of it, Joey had used the term two days ago. She strained to recall the meaning. It came to her.

The newspaper was paid a minimum fee to run the full-page ad. They also received a bonus for each person who responded to the ad. The better the response, the more money the newspaper stood to make. These kinds of advertising partnerships were perfectly legal. Joey had said so himself. But—connecting the dots—in this case it formed an added conflict of interest.

Suppress the news—make a buck. Their editorial content was being driven by the advertising dollars.

So much for freedom of the press.

Like a puzzle, the pieces were falling into place, and Jodi didn't like the picture they created. Armed with this new revelation, Jodi marched over to see her boss.

"Marge said you wanted to see me?" Jodi said, standing in the doorway to Joey's office. A copy of that morning's *Montgomery Times* was tucked under her arm. She held the cassette tape in her hand.

"Have a seat," Joey said, waving to the chair with his pen.

Jodi moved to the chair. She thought he seemed formal, yet polite—which was precisely what concerned her. Joey was usually warm. At the moment, like a highly charged energy field, his body language was giving off major negative energy. Come to think of it, she had felt the unnerving vibes the moment she approached his door.

She tried to sound upbeat. "So, what's up?"

"I just got a call from an irate client."

Jodi's heart skipped a beat. It had to be Dr. Graham.

"He says you made quite a scene this morning at his place of business."

"Well, see, I—"

Joey held a finger to his mouth. "Shh. I assured him you were *not* on an assignment from this paper and that you would be relieved of your duties."

"Huh?"

"Plain English? As much as I hate to do this, you're fired, Jodi."

She felt like she'd been smacked in the face with a wet rag. "For what?"

"Insubordination, for starters."

"I . . . I don't get it. Aren't you going to even hear my side of the story?"

He folded his arms together. "Who owns this paper?"

"You do."

"Who is the editor in chief?"

"That would be you, but—"

"But what? *I* decide the stories we pursue—not you. End of story. If I were you, maybe in the future I'd be more careful to follow directives. Now I'd like for you to clear out your desk. Roxanne will mail your final paycheck. I wish things didn't have to end this way."

Jodi felt as if hot flames were blazing around the edges of her ears. Her face, like a solar flare, sizzled. Jodi stood and walked to the front of his desk.

"What are you so afraid of, Mr. Stephano?"

He formed a tepee with his hands, tapping his fingertips together. "In this case, I'm primarily concerned about the legal action Dr. Graham has threatened—"

"Really?" she said, unfolding the paper. She dropped the paper face-down on the center of his desk, showing the clinic's ad on the back page. "Remember your advice to follow my nose? Well, I say this stinks like a real conflict of interest."

"You have no right to—"

"And another thing," Jodi said, barely able to contain the pent-up fire erupting from inside. "Your buddy, Dr. Graham, the very one Gus has been warning us about, was about to give me the full treatment this morning—and I'm not even pregnant."

"You expect me to believe that?"

Jodi held out the tape. "I recorded everything . . . including his attempt to cover it up."

Joey's eyes widened. "Jodi, let me have that tape."

She laughed. "Excuse me?"

He leaned forward and lowered his voice. "You're in way over your head. If what you say is true, the only way I can protect your legal interests is to present that tape as evidence to our lawyers."

Jodi looked at Joey and then at the tape. There was no question Dr. Graham would probably sue. He was an out-of-control madman as far as she was concerned. And, on the other hand, why shouldn't she trust Joey? Sure, maybe he had worked a sweet advertising deal with the clinic. That didn't mean he was a crook. He certainly wasn't in the same league as Dr. Graham.

Jodi bit her lip and started to hand him the tape.

In the back of her head, she heard Gus saying, *Not the wrong people . . . give it to the right people.*

She stopped.

"Jodi, give me the tape."

"Yeah, well, you know what? I think not . . . end of story."

Through the window in his office, Joey watched as Jodi cleared her desk. She walked to the front door for the last time, head tilted down. He picked up the phone and placed a call to a private number he had been given.

"It's Joey."

"Where's the cassette?"

Joey said, "She has it. She refused to hand it over."

Dr. Graham swore. "Tell me. Has Gus mailed you . . . anything, recently?"

"I haven't seen today's mail," Joey said. "Hold on a minute."

"Make it quick; I haven't got all day."

Joey raised an eyebrow. He put the doctor on hold and called for Marge.

"Hey, Marge, any crazy notes from Gus lately?"

She looked over the bridge of her glasses. "No. Not for you . . . Jodi got a small package."

"When?"

"Just now. She's probably got it with her," Marge said. She placed a hand on her hip. "Listen, Joey, not that it's my business, but she's such a nice kid—"

"Can't talk now, Marge," Joey said, ducking back into his office. He grabbed the phone. "I'm told Jodi got something from Gus today. Can't say what it was."

"I see."

Joey had to ask. "Is there a problem?"

Dr. Graham laughed. "Not anymore. By tonight, two rats will be sailing into the great beyond."

"Is that really necessary?" Joey asked.

Another laugh. "Depends on your point of view," Dr. Graham said and then hung up.

Joey waited a moment and then reached over to click off a tape recorder of his own.

⌢

The tears streaming down Jodi's face stung. She'd never been fired from anything before. What would she tell her dad and mom? She remembered how they had been so proud of her for landing the job. How could she explain this?

The fact that Joey wasn't interested in hearing her side of things hurt deeply. She had admired his years of experience, his vision for the paper, and she enjoyed being on the team—as Joey had called it. So much for teamwork.

And, after confronting Dr. Graham, to be fired today of all days, was a huge embarrassment.

She had failed Faith, too. Jodi had hoped this story would somehow help Faith and Pastor Morton save their home. What chance did she have of doing that now?

Jodi put the rest of her things in the backseat. When she closed the rear door, she noticed her back tire was as flat as a pancake. She squatted down for a closer look and, within seconds, saw a two-inch gash in the sidewall.

"Isn't that just perfect," she said to herself, reaching out to touch the wound.

A male voice said, "Flat tire, Jodi?"

Jodi recognized her name but not the voice. She looked up,

shielding her eyes against the sun. The last thing she remembered was a large, thick hand holding a handkerchief against her mouth.

She blacked out.

◡

"Looks like . . . the wrong people . . . found you."

Jodi's eyes blinked open, but she remained in the dark. That voice. That smell. Both were strangely familiar. Gus? Was she dreaming? Was she dying? What had she done? Where was she, anyway? Why was she here?

Did Gus do this to her? Nothing made sense.

One by one, the various parts of her body reported in. Everything hurt. Her head pounded. Her neck, sore. Her arms, numb. Her legs, like pins and needles. Her ankles, tied with thick, hairy ropes, chaffed and swollen. Her wrists, bound together.

In the darkness, she tried to speak. It was then that her mouth reported that a dirty rag, probably used to check someone's oil before it was discarded, was now sandwiched between her teeth. At least the gag stuffed in her mouth wasn't shoved down so far as to block off her ability to breathe.

Still, her lungs felt raw, charred, and inflamed as if they'd been left out in the sun too long without sunscreen. Jodi tried to push aside both her fears and the present discomfort to size up her situation—which, all signs indicated, was growing worse by the moment.

Now, more alert, a new set of sensations registered. She heard the drone of an engine. She felt herself swaying about the same time she heard water lapping against the side of the wall behind her back.

A boat? Whose boat? Where were they going?

Gus spoke again, as if able to read her mind. "Vic's boat . . . going to the ocean . . . to swim . . . a long swim. Miss Jodi . . . can you swim?"

She knew she should be panicking, but she didn't have the strength. In her mind she prayed, *God, please . . . I really need you.* She passed out again.

∽

Marge walked over to Joey's office. "Knock, knock," she said, standing in his doorway. With her left arm, she cradled her purse and a small yellow package.

Joey hung up the phone and waved her in.

"Actually, boss, it's almost four o'clock," Marge said, fiddling with an earring. "Yesterday, you said I could scoot by four. I got to go to my doctor's office, remember?"

Joey gave her a blank stare.

"That means, I'm leaving now, okay?"

Joey nodded and then reached for the phone. "Have fun."

"What's fun about going to the doctor's?" She turned to leave. "Oh, one more thing I almost forgot."

Joey looked back up. "I hope it makes my day."

"I don't know about that," Marge said. "But it looks like Jodi left this package from Gus in her bottom drawer. Want me to mail it to her?"

His eyes widened. "Give it here. I'll take care of that."

Marge handed him the package. As she left, she said over her shoulder, "If it's chocolate, save me some."

"Marge," he said, "if it's what I think it is, I'll buy you a whole case of Godiva."

Joey tore through the wrapping like a kid on Christmas Eve and retrieved a videotape. A low whistle escaped his lips. For a long moment he stared at it as if, like a mirage, the tape would suddenly vanish. "So, there really is a video?" he said under his breath. His heart began a happy dance in his chest.

He swiveled around in his chair, faced a thirteen-inch TV/VCR combo unit, and shoved the tape into its mouth. The screen jumped to life. He adjusted the volume so as not to be overheard elsewhere in the building. He sat forward on the edge of his chair as the first images filled the monitor.

The tape, he discovered, was seven minutes long. Seven of the most horrific minutes he'd ever witnessed in his life. He wiped the palms of his hands on his pants, ejected the tape, and shut off the system. For a full minute, Joey sat in silence.

He reached for the phone and dialed a number.

"Yes?"

"I've got Gus's videotape, Dr. Graham."

"How in the—"

"I'd like to propose a deal," Joey said, cutting him off. "Let's say it's a limited-time offer."

"I don't have time for games—"

"Oh, this is not a game, I assure you," Joey said.

"If you think you can blackmail me—"

"Again, Dr. Graham, you speak too hastily," Joey said. "I fully intend to give it to you, no strings attached."

"Well, then, bring it over here—"

Joey shook his head. "Now that's going to be a problem, Vic. Can I call you Vic?"

"You can call me whatever you want. Just get me that videotape."

"Fine. Here's the deal. I want to meet you at your boat in, say, forty-five minutes?"

Silence. Then, "Why there?"

"Let's just say I had such a good time," Joey said, "I figured it would be fun to do an encore, Vic. Can I put you down for five o'clock, dockside?"

"My time constraints are such that—"

"Victor, I watched the tape," Joey said. "If this falls into the wrong hands, you'll spend the rest of your life in a ten-foot-square cell. End of story."

"Five it is," Dr. Graham said.

The line went dead in Joey's ear. He dialed another number.

"Nine-one-one operator. What is the nature of your emergency?"

"I'd like to report a murder in progress."

Jodi was awakened by a sharp pull of the duct tape that covered her mouth. Her surroundings blinked into focus. As the cobwebs in her mind melted away, she realized the man leaning over her was Joey. Like a cornered cat, Jodi hunched her back and tried to back away from him. She wanted to scream for help, but her throat was still too dry.

"Listen, Jodi, everything is going to be all right," Joey said, removing the bindings from around her wrists.

A police officer, bending down as he walked into the compartment, appeared by Joey's side.

Jodi managed to swallow and then said, "He's . . . one of them."

"Relax, Miss Adams. Everything is under control."

Her head snapped back and forth. "No . . . no . . . he and Dr. Graham . . . they . . ."

The officer helped her up. "Come with me, ma'am."

"Keep him"—she pointed at Joey—"keep him away from me."

Joey followed two steps behind. "Listen, Jodi—"

She ignored him. "Officer, where am I?"

The policeman said, "This boat is registered to a Dr. Victor Graham, ma'am—and another thing. If Mr. Stephano here hadn't called us, you and Gus Anderson would probably not have lived to see another day."

Jodi swallowed hard. "I don't understand. My ex-boss," she said, her eyes narrowing, "he's got some little financial kickback scheme with Dr. Graham. He fired me because I was getting too close to the truth."

"Jodi, I don't expect you to believe me, at least not right now," Joey said. "The real reason I fired you was because I didn't want you to blow my cover."

"Your cover? What in the world are you talking about?"

Joey flashed his white teeth. "About a month before you came to work for us, Gus stopped by with one of his little letters—"

"Like the one I got?"

"More or less," Joey said. "He brought several different ones, each a slight variation of the others."

As the officer led the way off the boat and to the dock, Joey added, "Anyway, like I always say, follow your nose." He tapped the side of his beak. "I dug around and started to find there was more fact than fiction in Gus's story. Next thing I knew, you arrived on the scene and Gus gave you a letter like mine, with one big difference."

Jodi hooked her hair behind one ear.

"In your letter," Joey said, "he mentioned that he had a videotape of Dr. Graham suffocating a set of fully viable twins. Proof of a double homicide is enough to panic anyone—especially Dr. Graham."

"So," Jodi said, "when I started nosing around the clinic, you thought it could blow things between you and Dr. Graham?"

"Exactly." Joey held out a series of photographs for Jodi to see.

She flipped through them one by one. "But, now, I don't get it. These are pictures of you taking money from him. Like I said, you're on the take."

"Jodi, I paid a photographer to shadow me. Call it a hunch, but I figured Dr. Graham might just try to influence our coverage. I also wanted to see how far he'd go to cover up this thing—"

"Which is why Gus and I were about to go, like, swimming?"

Joey nodded. "You got it."

"One question?"

"Sure."

Jodi said, "What took you so long to get here?"

"Things had to fall into place. You see that squad car over there?" he said, pointing to the parking lot.

"Yeah."

"They're about to throw the book at Dr. Graham and his two thugs. Kidnapping and attempted murder," Joey said. "You're one lucky girl."

Jodi punched him lightly in the arm. "Luck had nothing to do with it. Let's say it was a God thing. Oh, and, by the way, where's Gus?"

"He's been rushed to Philadelphia Memorial Hospital," Joey said. "When we found you, he'd already been there for at least a day and was pretty dehydrated."

"Gosh, will he make it?"

"He'll do fine. They actually have soap there that can clean up someone as filthy as Gus."

They laughed. "And another thing, Jodi. You're a remarkable reporter."

That surprised her. "Do I get my job back?"

"Better than that," Joey said. "If you feel up to it, I'll work with you tonight to write the cover story for tomorrow."

"For real?" Jodi grabbed his arm and looked him in the eye. "You mean it?"

"Yup. End of story."

Stan bounded up the steps to Faith Morton's home and, with a knuckle, rapped three times on the screen door. In the other hand he held a bouquet of flowers. A folded-up copy of the newspaper was tucked under his arm. Pastor Morton came to the door carrying a cup of coffee.

"Stan, I see you haven't forgotten where we live."

"Hey, Pastor. I've got great news . . . I mean, seriously rockin' news."

He sipped his coffee, then cleared his throat. "I'm unfamiliar with 'seriously rockin' news,' but come in and we'll give a listen," Pastor Morton said, holding open the door.

Stan couldn't contain himself. "Can I tell Faith at the same time?"

"Whatever this news is, son, I hope it's contagious. We sure could use a lift around here," Pastor Morton said. He motioned to Stan to follow him down a short hall. "Honey, you up for some company? Stan's here."

A pause, then Faith said, "Okay, come in."

Faith lay in bed, propped up against the headboard. An open Bible rested on a pillow across her lap. The color in her skin had returned, and her hair was damp but combed as if she was just out of the shower.

Stan crossed over to her bedside and extended the flowers. "From us."

"Gosh, how sweet, Stan . . . but who's us?"

"I'm not sure how well you know Jodi Adams and Heather Barnes from school—"

"Sort of."

"Anyway, they've been praying for you—correction, we've been praying for you—"

"Me?"

Stan smiled. "Ever since you went into the hospital."

"So, Stan," Pastor Morton said, standing on the opposite side of the bed. "What's this, as you say, "rockin' news" all about?"

"Right. It's just this. . . . Read it for yourself."

Stan unfolded a copy of the *Montgomery Times* newspaper and placed it on Faith's lap. The headline, in three-inch, bold-faced type, read: BLACK FRIDAY.

Faith picked it up and started to read. "'When Faith Morton walked into the Total Choice Medi-Center, she thought she was in good hands. Nothing could have been further from the truth. For Faith, that Friday was the day her nightmare began and will probably always be remembered as Black Friday.'" Faith put down the newspaper for a second. She looked at Stan and then her dad. "No way . . . oh my gosh . . . this is about me? About that whacko doctor?"

"Isn't it awesome?" Stan said. "Jodi, with some help from her boss, wrote the story."

"Very cool," Faith said, skimming through the article.

Pastor Morton adjusted his glasses. "Stan, I don't know what to say."

"Wait 'til I tell you the best part," Stan said. He reached over the bed, flipped to page two, and then pointed. "Here. At the end. The editor told Jodi it would be cool to let readers donate money to help you pay for those medical bills."

Faith blinked. "I'm so shocked. Look, Daddy, maybe we won't have to sell the house." She held the section up for him to read.

"I don't get it," Pastor Morton said, visibly touched. "Why are they doing all of this for us?"

"I guess it's a human interest story or whatever," Stan said. "Okay, that, plus Jodi and I have been praying for some kind of miracle—"

Faith put a hand on Stan's arm. "It's so weird to hear you talk about praying."

Stan laughed. "Yeah, well, I'm still getting used to it myself. But, we've been praying for something else, too."

Faith raised an eyebrow.

Stan scratched the end of his chin. "See, Faith, we've been praying that your name would be more than just a name. It would be something you have inside."

Faith raised a finger. "Hold on. I think I know where you're going with this, and I don't want you to say another word, Stan."

Stan blushed. "I . . . I didn't mean to be—"

"Shh," Faith said. She turned to her dad. "Dad, I've been doing a lot of thinking this past week. Since that's, like, about all you can do in the hospital, besides watching TV."

Pastor Morton removed his glasses and placed his hands in his pockets without saying a word.

"Well, Dad, I was trying to think of why I never went along with everything you taught on Sundays," she said. She ran her fingers through her hair. "I don't mean to hurt you, Dad, but you've been so busy saving the world, it felt like most of the time you seemed to overlook our little corner of it. Guess I resented the church for taking you away from me so much."

Pastor Morton took her hand. "Faith, oh, Faith. I'm so sorry, I—"

"Shh," Faith said gently. "There's something I want to say. I read right here," she said, moving the paper aside and then picking up her Bible. "It's in, like, 1 John 1:9. Anyway, it says, 'If we confess our sins, he is faithful and just and will forgive us our sins and purify us from all unrighteousness.'"

Faith laid the Bible down. "I must have heard you quote that verse a hundred times since I was a kid, Dad. But now that I see how much I've blown it, I really do want to get right with God."

Stan looked at Pastor Morton. They exchanged a smile.

"How about Stan, here, doing the honors," Pastor Morton said, his eyes moist.

Stan waved him off. "Are you kidding? I'd probably blow it."

Faith squeezed her dad's hand. "C'mon, Dad."

"Honey, you have no idea how happy this makes me," Pastor Morton said, holding Faith's hand. He reached for Stan's hand, too, forming a circle. "Jesus, you say in your Word that you went to the cross, crowned with nothing more than thorns, and died. What a miracle when three days later you rose again. You died and now live so that each of us in this room can be changed and inherit eternal life."

Faith added, "And, Jesus, please come into my heart and take away my sin. Amen."

Stan said, "And I thought I had rockin' news. Faith, this is beyond awesome. . . . Wait until I tell Jodi."

S ome of the events described in this novel may appear to be too shocking to be true. Some will insist these things couldn't happen—certainly not in the United States of America.

Nothing could be further from the truth.

In reality, this account is based on a true story, many months of careful research, and interviews from those who previously worked, as Stan said, "on the dark side."

At the same time, there are many hurting people who, like Faith, made a choice they now deeply regret. If you are one of them, there's great news. A loving God longs to forgive and heal you. "Though your sins are like scarlet, they shall be as white as snow; though they are red like crimson, they shall be as wool" (Isaiah 1:18 NKJV).

Jesus invites you to embrace his grace. As Jodi said, it's a gift from God we don't deserve, can't earn or buy, and is free for the asking.

—TIM LAHAYE and BOB DEMOSS

THE AUTHORS WOULD LIKE TO EXTEND
THEIR APPRECIATION TO:

Tim Bergeron, Carol Everett, Carole Griffin, Greg Johnson,
Phil Keaggy, Don Lehrbaum, Ami McConnell, and Rebecca Wilson.

A special thanks to Bob's wife, Leticia, and daughter Carissa,
as well as Sharon DeMoss, and Robert and Dora DeMoss
for their constant feedback, prayers, and support.

I t was 10:33 P.M. Friday night. A seventeen-year-old girl lay curled in the fetal position on the second level of an abandoned warehouse in downtown Philadelphia. Though her eyes were slammed shut, in her mind she could see herself hovering, phantomlike, above her body.

The dark, rat-infested room where she lay crumpled on the floor spun out of control to the pulsating sounds she could hardly miss, yet couldn't fully hear. A high-pitched frequency, like a carpenter bee looking for a place to drill, whirled in her right ear. She wanted to swat at the source of this annoyance, but her right arm remained unresponsive. Her legs felt numb, and she discovered that they, too, refused to respond when commanded to move.

Her throat was dry—yet somehow was as tacky as flypaper. She tried to swallow but was incapable of that simple task.

Her lungs, attempting to pull in the thick night air through her pierced nose, were greeted by a nasty mix of fumes and dust. She longed for just one full, clean breath of fresh air.

She struggled to fight back the waves of panic. What was happening to her? Why did her guts feel as if they were about to explode? Why was she perspiring when she felt so cold? Why was she wearing pixie wings and pink sneakers?

Just then, her tongue reported something was jammed into her mouth. Her teeth clamped down on its rubbery surface and wouldn't let go. With some effort, she forced her mind to focus. Like the headlight of an approaching car on a foggy night, a dim recognition of the object cut a path through the haze in her head.

A pacifier. How odd.

As she struggled to make sense of the competing sensory input, she was vaguely aware of an acidic bile traveling between her stomach and throat. The bitter, brownish-yellow fluid ejected by her liver, like hot lava pushing its way against the surface, battled for immediate release.

More than anything she wanted to vomit.

Then got her wish.

Her mind raced in slow motion, searching for an explanation. Maybe it was a touch of food poisoning.

*No. No. NO!*

*Look what you've done. Face it. You screwed up, big time. What are you on?* She was fairly certain the voice echoing inside her head, though familiar-sounding, wasn't her own.

Or was it? It was so difficult to tell.

Was she dead? Was this the last stop before hell? She knew she wasn't ready to die. Certainly hadn't planned to die.

She knew she couldn't speak, yet a feeble voice from someplace inside whispered, *Oh God . . . if you're there, I could use a little help right about now. I . . . Jesus, I . . .*

A sharp pain seared her left arm, interrupting her cry for help. The limb, which had been sandwiched between her body and the hardwood floor, throbbed and demanded to be recognized. She remembered something about a needle, a tranquilizer . . .

With a head full of unanswered questions, she passed out—again.

*Also Available in the* Soul Survivor *Series*

## THE MIND SIEGE PROJECT

In the tradition of MTV's "The Real World", eight high school juniors volunteer for a week on a houseboat in the name of experimental education. Rosie Meyer, the former Olympic silver medallist turned social studies teacher, dreams of her students learning first-hand the realities of tolerance and diversity. And learn they do. Although the students sail for a single week, the issues faced, the truths uncovered, and the lessons learned leave them changed for a lifetime.

## ALL THE RAVE

More than 15,000 ravers have gathered for a 72-hour dance party at the waterfront warehouse in Philadelphia. Kat is strung out on drugs and next to her lies the body of a dead boy who overdosed; Heather falls in love with a college freshman who threatens to leave her with nothing but feelings of rejection and serious regret. Experiencing firsthand the dangers of an unguarded heart, the girls are forced to reevaluate God's true place in their lives.

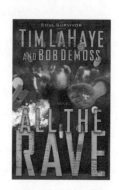

## THE LAST DANCE

Spring is about to give way to summer and love is in the air. Heather Barnes has found the guy of her dreams, John Knox, a senior at a nearby high school whom she met in a Christian chat room. Although Heather has never actually "met" John in person, she plans to go to the prom with him against the advice of her best friend, Jodi Adams. Soon, Heather will discover John's true identity. Can Jodi, Bruce, and Kat rescue Heather before it's too late or will the prom be her last dance?

## BLACK FRIDAY

Jodi Adams has landed her dream job as a summer intern at the local city paper, The Montgomery Times. This killer summer job will launch her senior year with a bang as she goes after the hard angle on an investigative piece on area hospitals. But when Jodi's reporting reveals information her employer doesn't want to hear—much less publish—Jodi and Stan Taylor find that the information trail is vanishing before their eyes. Lives are at stake, and it looks like theirs could be next.

W Publishing Group™
www.wpublishinggroup.com